A Bullet for Lawless

When ex-lawman Ben Lawless took a bushwhacker's bullet that almost killed him he knew the man who'd shot him and he also knew that the bushwhacker never missed: so why was Lawless still breathing?

With rancher Veronica Ketchum to thank for his life, Lawless decides to return the favour and back Veronica in her battle with land-grabbing cattle-baron, Stillman J. Stadtlander. Their paths have crossed before and Lawless is no fool: he cannot take on Stadtlander's gunhawks alone. He enlists old friends, Drifter and the enigmatic Gabriel Moonlight, and just for good measure calls in Latigo Rawlins, the very man who had him bushwhacked. . . .

A Bullet for Lawless

Steve Hayes

A Black Horse Western

ROBERT HALE · LONDON

© Steve Hayes 2014
First published in Great Britain 2014

ISBN 978-0-7198-1373-3

Robert Hale Limited
Clerkenwell House
Clerkenwell Green
London EC1R 0HT

www.halebooks.com

Typeset by
Derek Doyle & Associates, Shaw Heath
Printed and bound in Great Britain by
CPI Antony Rowe, Chippenham and Eastbourne

This one is for you, Brooke

PROLOGUE

After they'd shot his horse out from under him in Canon de Oro, a deep, sheer-sided gorge in the mountains west of Palomas, Mexico, they did what he hadn't expected: pursued him across the border into the United States.

That was when Lawless realized just how determined they were to hunt him down and kill him.

Now, two days later, he watched as three *pistoleros* rode along the arroyo toward him, the bright sunlight reflecting off the silver *conchos* adorning their sombreros and fancy, high-pommel saddles. Chambering a round into his Winchester '86, he rested the barrel on the rock in front of him and centered his sights on the lead rider, Ernesto Sanchez.

At sixty, Ernesto was old for a *pistolero*. A small, lean, dignified man with silver hair, fierce dark eyes and a white drooping mustache that hid the corners of his stern, thin-lipped mouth, he possessed little humor and seldom smiled. But he knew what honor was, a rare trait for a *pistolero*, and had never shot anyone who wasn't facing him.

Lawless knew him well. A year ago, he and several other *gringo* gunmen had been hired to help Ernesto and his *vaqueros* drive off rustlers who were stealing cattle from ranchers, especially Don Francisco Diego – a wealthy *hacendado* whom everyone called *Patron*.

It was because of those months of riding together, when he and Ernesto had had each other's back, that Lawless' conscience wouldn't allow him to shoot his old friend from behind cover like a common bush-whacker.

Waiting until the three riders were almost level with him, Lawless stepped from behind the rocks and confronted them, rifle aimed at Ernesto's heart.

'*Parad alli!*'

The startled Mexicans reined up their slathered horses, the two men flanking Ernesto inching their hands toward their six-guns.

'Go ahead,' Lawless said grimly. 'It'll give me an excuse to kill you.'

The gunmen froze, their angry expressions warning him that they were merely biding their time.

'Truth is, *hombres*, but for Ernesto, here, you'd be dead meat right now.'

The gunmen glared balefully at him, hands frozen at their sides.

Keeping his eyes on them, Lawless spoke to Ernesto. 'You lost, *amigo*?'

'This you know better than to ask,' the old *pistolero* replied.

'Still got it, huh?'

'Like my soul, it will be with me until I die.'

Lawless smiled, pleased. The compass had belonged to his grandfather, a renowned New England sailing skipper, and it had given Lawless great pleasure to give it to Ernesto as a parting gift.

But that was then; now was now.

'Then I reckon you know you're in New Mexico, *amigo*.'

It is with great sadness that I find myself here,' Ernesto said.

'I feel the same sadness,' Lawless said, adding: 'The *patron* must be *muy enojado* if he told you to follow me across the border.'

'What did you expect? Wouldn't you be very angry if someone stole what you valued most?'

'His daughter?'

'Her heart.'

'Killing me won't get that back. Josefina's been tryin' to get away from that domineering old buzzard ever since her mother died. Everyone knows that. If it hadn't been me, it would've been someone else.'

' "Someone else" did not work for him or betray his trust.'

'Trust? Don Diego doesn't even know the meanin' of the word.'

'Nevertheless, he is her father and it is a father's responsibility to make sure his daughter does not live in shame.'

'I wanted to marry her, he knew that.'

'You are not of her faith. It still would have been shameful.'

'And keepin' her locked up like a condemned prisoner isn't? *Madre de Dios*, Ernesto, Josefina isn't one of his prize bulls. She's a beautiful, passionate young woman. Surely you don't want her to spend her whole life lookin' out of a barred windo—' Lawless broke off as the gunman to his left went for his pistol.

Lawless pumped a round into him. Even as the man pitched from his saddle, Lawless quickly swung the rifle to the right and fired again, this time knocking the other gunman from his horse.

He then turned back to Ernesto. 'Don't move, *compadre*. Last thing I want to do is kill you.'

The old *pistolero* smiled sadly at him.

'We do what we must,' he said regretfully – and jerked his iron.

Lawless shot him, twice, both rounds ripping through Ernesto's heart.

Ernesto's pistol fell from his limp hand and he slid from the saddle.

Dismayed, Lawless dropped his rifle and kneeled beside his dead friend. He'd had no choice but to kill the old *pistolero* – Ernesto, at any age, was too dangerous to risk wounding him – but that didn't lessen Lawless' pain. There was now a hole in his heart that would never heal. Cradling the old man against him, he looked into Ernesto's dark, empty-staring eyes.

'Damn you,' he whispered. 'Why'd you force me to kill you?'

High overhead a hawk screeched.

Lawless looked up, squinting in the bright sunlight,

and saw the raptor circling lazily overhead on the thermals. Were the Apaches right, he wondered? Could a hawk really guide a man's soul to the Spirit World?

By God, he surely hoped so.

Searching Ernesto's pockets, he found what he was looking for and took it out. As big and heavy as a Hamilton pocket watch, the silver-cased compass felt good in his hand. Momentarily he sensed his dead grandfather was near. He smiled without realizing and fondly tucked the compass into the breast pocket of his jacket. Its lumpy weight felt comforting; as if the compass belonged there.

He heard the hawk screech again. But when he looked up the bird was gone.

Rising, Lawless carried Ernesto to the rocks. There, he gently laid the body on the warm sand, drew his knife and started digging the *pistolero's* grave.

It took twenty minutes to dig a hole that was deep enough to bury his friend, and another ten to scrape the loose dirt back over the corpse. When he was finished, Lawless was dripping sweat. He added to the pounding of his heart by carrying several large rocks to the grave where he placed them atop the mound of dirt so that scavengers couldn't dig up the body.

'*Descanse en paz, mi amigo,*' he said quietly. With a heavy sigh he walked back to Ernesto's horse. There, he turned and looked at the grave, at the same time hoping that his friend would indeed rest in peace, and then swung up on to the fine-boned, pureblood

Colonial Spanish mare. The horse, a line-backed dun with a gold-gray body, dark face and dark mane and tail, adjusted to his weight and at the touch of Lawless' spurs, trotted forward.

That's when a rifle shot rang out.

Lawless felt a hammer-like blow strike his left temple. Lights exploded behind his eyes. Blackness followed and he slid from the saddle.

A short, slim man stepped out from the rocks, holding a Henry repeating rifle. He was dressed similar to the other, deceased Mexicans but the face under the high-crowned sombrero belonged to a boyishly handsome, blond-haired *gringo* whose strange, amber-colored eyes were devoid of emotion.

He stared down at Lawless, who lay sprawled on his face, motionless, blood from the bullet wound reddening the dirt. He showed no remorse or satisfaction, and made no attempt to see if Lawless was alive or dead. He merely removed his sombrero, placed it on the ground beside Lawless' head and whistled softly.

A rangy golden sorrel trotted out from behind the rocks and stopped beside the man. Unfastening the cinch strap, he removed the fancy, high-pommeled Mexican saddle from the horse's back and dropped it beside the sombrero. He did the same with the silver-*concho*-adorned bridle. Finally, free of all association with Mexico, he grasped the long, flowing mane and vaulted on to the sorrel's back.

Humming tunelessly, Latigo Rawlins rode north in the direction of Santa Rosa.

CHAPTER ONE

Lawless stirred restlessly, his mind in a blank daze. He felt something cool and damp placed on his forehead. His mind cleared for a moment. Immediately his head throbbed with a dizzying pain, especially along his left temple. He had no idea where he was or what had happened to him – other than vaguely remembering a violent blow to his head on the same side as the pain was now.

He heard muffled voices talking in the distance. He tried to listen to them, to understand what they were saying, but his mind refused to focus. The words were all jumbled together, making no sense.

Then blackness returned and Lawless remembered no more.

When he regained consciousness, his temple still throbbed painfully but the dizziness was gone. He could no longer hear voices; only a horse nickering in the distance.

Lawless opened his light-gray eyes. Everything was blurred. He closed his eyes again, waited a few

moments, then reopened them. Momentarily everything was still blurred – then he heard the horse
nickering again, closer, somewhere outside, and
blinked several times. Abruptly, everything came into
focus and he realized he was lying in bed in a room
that was dark save for the sunlight entering between
the partly closed drapes.

He looked up and saw a beamed ceiling, the
adobe between the beams stained yellow by rain
leaks. Glancing around, he saw several sepia pho-
tographs on the oak-paneled walls depicting ranch
life: hard-bellied cowboys, cigarettes dangling from
their lips, gathered outside a log bunkhouse; punchers branding a calf on open range; ranch-hands
leaned against a corral fence, watching a rider breaking a wild mustang; the same men gathered around
a camp fire; and a much larger photo of a middle-
aged, jut-jawed, gimlet-eyed, mustachioed rancher
with his arms held in a fatherly, almost overly protec-
tive fashion about a young man – no, Lawless
corrected himself, a young woman.

Curious, he studied her carefully. About sixteen,
she wore a man's shirt, jeans and boots and her hat
was pushed back off her head, revealing boyishly
short hair that was pale as winter sunshine.

Though she wasn't the prettiest girl he'd ever
seen, there was an innocent, vivacious, farm-fresh
look about her that Lawless found very appealing.
Surprised by how she'd affected him, he was wondering who she was when a wave of nausea swept
through him. He closed his eyes and waited for the

dizziness to stop.

Just then he heard the door open. Opening his eyes, he saw someone approaching the bed. She looked familiar and he realized it was the same woman he'd seen in the photo – only now her hair was shoulder-length and he guessed she was three or four years older.

But she was still fresh-faced and appealing, and prettier in person than in the photo. Tanned by the sun, she had a splash of freckles across her pert nose, large hazel eyes and a smile that lit up dark corners.

She smiled now, delighted to find him awake, and sat on the bed beside him.

'So,' she teased, 'you've finally decided to rejoin the living?'

He nodded, the movement causing his left temple to throb painfully. He gently reached up to touch the sore spot and realized his head was bandaged.

'It's about time, mister. We were getting worried about you.'

'W-We?' Lawless heard himself say.

'Dr Shaw for one; me for another.'

Guessing that the doctor must have examined him while he was unconscious, Lawless silently waited for her to continue.

'How are you feeling now – any better?'

'*Sí, señorita.*'

'Doc says you're very lucky. A fraction closer and that bullet would have killed you.'

'If I was lucky,' Lawless said drily, 'I wouldn't have been shot at all.'

The woman laughed softly. 'I never thought of it that way.'

Lawless looked about him and then asked: '*¿Dónde estoy, por favor?*'

'Daddy's bedroom. It's all right,' she said as he looked concerned. 'My father doesn't need it anymore. He's – dead. Killed.'

Lawless' grim expression told her that he was sorry.

'Thanks,' she said as if he'd spoken. 'I still miss him a lot, but at least now he's with Mother again. And, truth is, that's all he ever wanted anyway – to be with Momma.' She paused, a faint flash of jealousy in her eyes that almost immediately vanished. 'I don't remember much about her,' she continued. 'The fever took her when I was only a toddler, but I know she loved me. . . .' She frowned, her gold-flecked, greenish-brown eyes filled with a mixture of sadness and anger. 'I don't mean to sound like a whining little girl, but losing your folks, even though their deaths were years apart, still hurts and' – she caught herself and shook her head crossly, as if scolding herself – 'Dammit, I vowed not to act like this anymore.'

'Like what?'

'A weak-kneed crybaby.'

'Missin' your folks, ma'am, don't mean you're weak or a crybaby.'

'You don't think so?'

'Not at all.'

'You're not just saying that to make me feel better?

16

No, of course you're not,' she said before he could reply. 'You're not that kind of man. Anybody with half an eye could tell that.'

He wasn't sure where this was leading, but said nothing.

'I'm glad you feel that way – about caring for loved ones, I mean.'

Lawless wondered why she cared what he thought, but again said nothing.

'Being a woman and knowing that men don't like weepy women, I've always felt that any show of emotion could be misconstrued as weakness . . . and the last thing I can afford to do is look weak before the hands. They need someone to lead them, to set an example, to act tough like Daddy always did when it came time to stand up against . . . oh, God,' she said, hearing herself, 'will you listen to me? Carrying on so in front of a perfect stranger. . . .' To hide her embarrassment, she removed the damp towel from his forehead, dipped it in a bowl of water on the bedside table, squeezed the excess water from it and replaced the towel on his brow. 'There, how's that feel?'

'*Muy bueno.*'

She studied him for a moment, puzzled. 'I don't mean to be rude, mister, but you're not Mexican, are you?'

Lawless shook his head.

'Then why do you keep lapsing into Spanish?'

He hadn't realized that that was what he'd been doing. 'Old habits die hard, I reckon.'

'Oh, do you live in Mexico?'

'Not anymore.'

She paused, studying him intently before continuing. 'Reason I ask is my men said they found you right at the border beside two dead *pistoleros* and a freshly dug grave. Said your horse had a fancy Mexican saddle on it, too.'

If she'd expected him to explain, she was disappointed because his blank expression told her nothing.

'It's none of my business, of course, but if someone's out to kill you, it wouldn't hurt to tell me. I could have the boys keep an eye out for any gunmen or . . . suspicious-looking strangers.'

'No need for that, ma'am.'

'Oh-h. Well, good. . . .' Though her eyes were full of questions, she changed the subject. 'Think you could eat something? Little broth, maybe? I've got some warming on the stove. . . .'

'Broth sounds good.'

'I'll bring you a bowl right away.'

'Be obliged if you'd tell me your name first.'

'Oh, gracious, where are my manners?' She offered him her hand. 'I'm Veronica Ketchum – though I prefer to be called Ronnie.' When he didn't say anything, she said: 'And what should I call you, Mr—?'

'No Mr. Just Lawless is fine.'

'Lawless? Interesting name. Very well, broth it is.' She started to leave.

'One last thing,' he said as she reached the door.

'Your men – the ones who found me – how'd they happen to be right at the border?'

'They were rounding up strays.'

'They see anyone else?'

'As a matter of fact, yes.'

'A shootist?'

'Could be. Boys said his holsters were tied down low. You know him?'

'Possible.'

'Then next time you see him, thank him. He most likely saved your life. If he hadn't told them where you were before he rode off, you'd be—'

'Wolf bait?'

'That or lunch for the buzzards. There was a bunch of them camped out around you when the boys rode up.'

'Guess it wasn't my day to die,' Lawless said, adding: 'This shootist, ma'am, did he say anything 'bout why he didn't help me himself?'

'Uh-uh. And my men never asked. They did say, however, that he was riding bareback, with just a rope halter – no bit, bridle, stirrups or anything.'

'They also mention what he looked like?'

'Small . . . hair the color of sawdust . . . nice-looking but . . . with odd, yellow-brown eyes – the kind that could easily throw a cold scare into you. Least, that's how the boys felt. That description fit anyone you know?'

'No,' Lawless lied. He then closed his eyes, ending the conversation.

Veronica shrugged and went out.

Lawless waited till her footsteps faded on along the hallway, then opened his eyes and stared at the ceiling.

So, he thought. *He had a chance to kill me and didn't . . . just creased me instead . . . that's not like Latigo. Not like him at all.*

What the hell was going on?

CHAPTER TWO

By mid-afternoon Lawless felt strong enough to get up. But Veronica wouldn't hear of it. Neither would Dr Shaw, who stopped by to check on his patient and to put on a fresh bandage. Together they convinced Lawless to remain in bed until the following morning.

Lawless, like all active men, hated to be bedridden. But though he never would have admitted it, he still felt weak and was glad of the chance to rest. He lay there dozing, slowly regaining his strength, until early evening when Veronica brought him his supper.

'I hope you feel well enough to eat,' she said, setting the tray across his lap. 'I'm not the world's best cook, but steak and potatoes beats the beans and rice and burned stew the boys are chowing down in the bunkhouse.'

'Looks wonderful,' Lawless said. Embarrassed by all the fuss, he started to add that she didn't have to wait on him like he was an invalid, but she silenced him with a brusque wave of her hand and hurried out. She didn't return until he had finished eating and then she served him a wedge of fresh-baked berry pie that she said was made by the cook, not her.

'Like I said earlier, cooking isn't my specialty. No, no,' she added, seeing his look of doubt. 'I'm serious, Lawless. If I'd baked that pie you'd be praying for me to leave so you could dump it out the window.'

Lawless chuckled.

'You should do that more often.'

'What?'

'Laugh – instead of acting so grim and serious all the time. Oh, I know you were shot and that must be awful, knowing someone actually tried to kill you, but you're safe now and among friends, and hopefully. . . .'

'Hopefully what?' he said when she didn't finish.

'Well, hopefully . . . you know . . . you'll get to like it here enough so that you won't want to move on.'

Lawless studied her a moment. He knew what he was going to say and was surprised that he found it difficult to say it. 'I appreciate all you've done for me, ma'am, but come mornin' I *will* be movin' on.'

'I see.'

'Don't reckon you do. While I been lyin' here I've had time to think, and I'm pretty sure now I know who it was who shot me—'

'—and you can't let him get away with it, even if it means turning down good wages and a chance to help someone who really needs helping. Only thing that matters to you is that you kill him—'

'Ma'am—'

'—proving to everyone how fast you are with a gun.'

'*Ma'am*,' he repeated, louder now, 'that ain't the reason I'm movin' on.'

'It isn't?'

'No, ma'am.'

She made a face. 'Could you please call me Ronnie? Ma'am makes me feel like a middle-aged spinster.'

Lawless smiled wryly. 'That's a thought never would come to me.'

'Thank you. But all flattery aside, why can't you stay and ramrod my outfit?'

'For the simple fact, Miss Ronnie, I've never punched cows for a livin' and I wouldn't be comfortable tryin' my hand at it now.'

'You wouldn't have to punch cows. I've got regular hands to do that.'

'Then what do you need me for?'

She hesitated, as if not sure if she should explain, and then released her indecision in a long, frustrated sigh.

'When the boys first brought you here, I asked them if they knew who you were. None of them did. But later that evening Matt Keegan, who worked here when Father was alive, told me that although he didn't know you, he did recognize the man who found you. Said he was a bounty hunter and a cold-blooded killer who once worked for Stillman J.

Stadtlander.'

Lawless didn't say anything, but the mention of New Mexico's most powerful and ruthless rancher hardened his eyes.

'Do you know Mr Stadtlander?'

'Not personally, no. But over the years I've seen him and his son, Slade, in Santa Rosa on occasion, though we never actually met.'

'I'd keep it that way, if I were you.'

'I intend to. After what he did to a friend of mine, he ain't the kind of *hombre* I want to shake hands with.'

Veronica looked interested. 'May I ask what happened?' Then, as Lawless hesitated: 'It's all right. You don't have to tell me if you don't want to.'

Lawless shrugged. 'Reckon it's no secret. My friend won a thoroughbred from Stadtlander in a poker game. He won it fair and square, but Stadtlander had big plans for the stallion and tried to buy him back. When my friend refused, rather than lose face, as well as the stallion, Stadtlander branded Gabe a horse thief. He bribed the sheriff to go along with him—'

'That'd be Sheriff Hansen?'

'Uh-uh. Before Will Hansen.'

'Oh, you mean Lonnie Forbes?'

Lawless nodded. 'It was Stadtlander's money and influence that got Forbes elected, and next thing Gabe knew he was facin' a rope. So he lit out for Mexico an' has been hidin' out there ever since.'

'Wait a minute,' Veronica exclaimed. 'Are you

24

talking about the outlaw, Mesquite Jennings?'

'How'd you know that?' asked Lawless, surprised.

'Daddy was friends with Ingrid Bjorkman and her daughter, Raven. Said Ingrid talked about Mesquite all the time, 'cept she called him by his real name – Gabriel something.'

'Moonlight?'

'Y-Yes, that's it.' Veronica shook her head in amazement. 'I guess it really is a small world – even out here in the southwest.'

'Reckon so. . . .' Lawless thought a moment before adding: 'What's your quarrel with Stadtlander?'

'He killed my father.'

'You mean he had one of his hired guns do it?'

'No. Personally. Just gunned Daddy down. That surprises you?' she added, reading his expression.

'Kind of. Stadtlander's many things, most of 'em bad, but I never pegged him for a murderer.'

'Legally, he isn't. He claimed it was self-defense. Said Daddy forced him into it, but that's a damned lie.'

'You were there?'

'No. I was here at the ranch. But that doesn't change the truth.'

'Second-hand truth, you mean?'

'I know my father. What he was capable of and what he would never do. That's enough truth for me.'

Rather than argue, Lawless let it slide. 'Where'd it happen?'

'Along the Lower Snake. That's a river that runs

through our property—'

'Yeah, I know.'

'Stadtlander's men kept driving our cows away from the water, so his cattle could drink. One day he and Daddy got into an argument over it and Stadtlander shot him. Claimed he had no choice. Said my father threatened him with a shotgun. Later, at the inquest, he changed it to a rifle, but that's only because Daddy's Winchester was found lying in the mud beside his body.'

'What about witnesses?'

'There were plenty – but they all ride for the Double S.'

'What about your men – where were they?'

'Rounding up our spooked cattle.'

'So they can't say what happened, either way?'

'Uh-uh. They just heard shots and when they came riding back, Daddy was already . . . dead.'

Lawless sighed, troubled.

'So, now that you know what I'm up against, will you help me fight Stadtlander? My men are loyal,' she added before Lawless could reply, 'perhaps even more than I've a right to expect. But they're wranglers and punchers plain and simple, and no match for the kind of men Stadtlander has working for him.'

'Gunslingers, you mean?'

'Exactly.'

'What about Sheriff Hansen?'

'He says he can't – won't act unless I've got proof that Stadtlander's men are stopping my cattle from reaching the river.'

'Why would they want to do that? Even in summer there's water enough for everyone.'

'You're missing the point. Stadtlander knows if my cows die of thirst, I'd be forced to sell this place. Then he'd buy it, just like he's bought up most of the other spreads around here. I know I sound like every other small-time rancher who's fighting to survive,' she said, seeing the doubt in Lawless' expression, 'but that doesn't mean I'm not telling the truth. When Father was alive Stadtlander tried to force him to sell our place several times and then threatened him when Daddy turned him down. 'Course, that's not how Stadtlander tells it. He claims he and Daddy signed a paper allowing him to water his cattle anywhere along the river in time of drought.'

'Have you seen this paper?'

'No. Neither has anyone else. Stadtlander swears he lost his copy of the contract and that Daddy's copy is with some lawyer they hired – which is another lie, 'cause no such lawyer exists. If he did, I'd surely know about it.' She sighed, helplessly. 'I've tried to hire gunmen who'd be willing to stand up to Stadtlander, but he always offers them twice what I can pay and they end up working for him.'

'Does the sheriff know about this?'

'Sure. But again it's my word against Stadtlander's. And since he's too smart to ever have his men do anything illegal when the sheriff's around, there's nothing Hansen can do about it – even though he's admitted to me, in private, that he knows

Stadtlander's guilty as hell.'

Lawless shrugged. 'Maybe you should consider selling – buyin' a spread somewhere else.'

'Never,' Veronica said angrily. 'My folks are buried on this land, and I sure as hell intend to be buried next to them. Wouldn't you feel the same way?' she added when Lawless didn't say anything.

'Possible.'

'Then will you help me?'

'Even if I agreed to, what makes you think I could make a difference?'

'Just a hunch.'

'Don't lie to me, Miss Ronnie.'

'All right,' she said. 'Truth is, my men don't wear tie-down holsters, or file the sights off their pistols so they won't snag during a fast-draw.'

'Don't miss much, do you?'

'I'm the one who put you to bed, remember?'

He didn't, but it explained her nosiness. 'Any other reason?'

'The company you keep – a known outlaw and a cold-blooded bounty hunter who, according to my men, is the fastest gun in the territory – maybe the whole southwest.'

'Who tried to *kill* me – 'case you've forgotten.'

'Odd you should bring that up. Sheriff Hansen, who rode out here yesterday after he heard about the shooting, has another explanation.'

'I'd like to hear it.'

'He thinks Latigo Rawlins missed you on purpose. Said if he'd meant to kill you, you'd be fertilizing wildflowers instead of nursing a head wound – which got me to thinking. Why would a deadly killer just graze you and ride off, then tell my hands exactly where they could find you so they could save your life?'

'If you're implyin' we're *amigos*,' Lawless said, 'maybe you can explain why he shot me in the first place?'

'I haven't figured that one out yet,' Veronica admitted, 'though I'm sure the answer's simple enough if I knew the whole story.'

She waited hopefully for him to explain. Instead, he sighed wearily.

'Forgive me,' she said, 'you're tired and need rest. Anyways, I've talked too much already.' She went to the door, paused and looked back at him. 'In the morning, if you still want to move on, you'll find that pureblood mare of yours in the corral behind the barn. The boys brought her in when they delivered you.' She was gone, the door closing quietly behind her before Lawless could respond.

He sighed again and leaned back against the pillows.

Stillman J. Stadtlander, Gabe Moonlight, Ingrid and Raven, Latigo Rawlins – why the hell couldn't the past stay buried and stop chewing on him?

CHAPTER THREE

Sleep didn't come easy that night.

Half of him wanted to help Veronica, the other half didn't. Trouble was the half that didn't had reason and logic on its side – something always hard to ignore when you were the type of man whose mainstay in life was common sense. On the other hand, trying to use common sense when you were burdened with chivalrous instincts, instincts that required a man to help *any* woman in distress, was asking for trouble from the get-go.

And Veronica wasn't just 'any' woman, Lawless reminded himself. She was a strong, brave, attractive young woman who genuinely needed his help against a powerful, ruthless enemy; an enemy that would use any means to get what he wanted – even a hangman's noose if necessary. Just ask Gabe Moonlight. What's more, if she continued to stand up to him, Stadtlander would have no trouble grinding her into the ground. In fact, he would most likely sleep all the better for it.

It was a dilemma that kept Lawless' mind spinning. He argued with himself until exhaustion took over and he drifted off without realizing.

Next thing he remembered was waking up to a rooster crowing. Groggy, he pulled on his jeans and boots and went into the kitchen. Dawn was breaking over the distant mountains and its pale-yellow light filtered in through the curtained window. Going to the sink, he pumped water into a chipped porcelain bowl. He splashed some over his face and bare upper body, the shock of the cold water chasing the last ounce of sleep from him. But his head still throbbed and when he pulled up the edge of the bandage, he could feel dried blood caked in the hair above his ear.

Still wondering why Latigo hadn't killed him, Lawless toweled himself off and returned to the bedroom. There he finished dressing and buckled on his gun-belt. There was a faint noise behind him. His back was to the door and he whirled around, gun jumping into his hand.

'It's just me,' Veronica said, holding the lighted candle up to her face.

'Sorry.' Lawless holstered his Colt, embarrassed by his edginess.

She smiled. ' "Old habits die hard"?'

'Reckon.'

'Coffee's ready.' Turning, she entered the kitchen, put the candle on the table by the window and went to the stove. There, she picked up the pot heating atop it and filled two mugs sitting nearby.

Lawless joined her. As she brought one mug to him, his frown made her say: 'You're not the only one with old habits, you know. Father liked his coffee early too.'

There was sadness in her voice and Lawless wasn't sure how to answer. He noticed a bowl of sugar on the table and helped himself to a spoonful. As he stirred his coffee, Veronica brought her cup to the table, sat and took a tiny cautious sip, winced, then blew on the coffee to cool it.

Lawless sat across from her. 'What else did he like?'

'My father?' She thought a moment. 'A good cigar. Honesty in anyone. The good feeling he got after a hard day's work. Simple things.'

Lawless studied her above his coffee cup. 'He was lucky to have you.'

She looked surprised, as if the thought had never occurred to her.

'*I* was lucky to have him. Even for only a short time. He made life whole for me.'

Lawless nodded, for a moment envying her, and sipped his coffee in silence.

'You've decided to move on, haven't you?' she said, not looking up.

'Seems like.'

She nodded, eyes still lowered so he wouldn't see her disappointment.

'Can't say as I blame you.'

Lawless took a gulp of coffee, silently cursing as it burned his tongue.

'I had no right to ask you in the first place. I know that now.'

Sensing she wasn't finished, he remained silent.

'Daddy always said I was too demanding – well, actually he said "pushy". And I guess I am. It's just. . . .' her voice trailed off.

Both sipped their hot coffee in silence.

'Look,' Lawless began.

'No, no,' she interrupted, 'you don't have to apologize. This isn't your fight. there's no reason to feel like you're obligated or—'

'I wasn't goin' to apologize, Miss Ronnie. An' I don't feel obligated.'

'Oh-h. . . .' She met his eyes for an instant; then, cheeks reddening, looked away. 'Isn't that just like me – jumping the gun, as always.'

'Is that what your pa used to tell you?'

She nodded. Kept her eyes lowered and idly stirred her coffee.

'Just 'cause he was your pa, doesn't mean he was always right.'

'But he was. I know that now. And if I hadn't been so damn headstrong, like Ma used to say—'

'Thought your ma died when you were still a toddler.'

'She did, but—'

'Your pa told you what she said?'

For a moment anger flashed in Veronica's green-gold eyes.

'What're you trying to say – that he made stuff up to suit him?'

His silence further angered her.

'Dammit, that's just not true,' she snapped. 'Ask anyone in town – they'll all tell you the same thing: that Daddy was a man of integrity whose word you could take to the bank.'

Lawless sipped his coffee. It was cooler now and he swilled it around inside his mouth so he could enjoy the taste of it, thinking as he did that other than tobacco, he liked coffee better than anything.

'Why don't you say something?' she demanded. 'If you've heard anything different about my father, then I insist you tell me. Because it's not only not true, it's unfair. He isn't here to defend himself and—'

He stopped her. 'I ain't heard anythin' about your pa. Truth is I never even heard anyone mention his name, good or bad.' Gulping down the last of his coffee, he rose, put his hat on and gave her a quick smile. 'I'd like to pay you for all your kindness, Miss Ronnie, but I'm worried you might take offense. . . .'

'I would,' she said, still angry, 'so don't you dare offer me anything.'

'Reckon I'll be leavin', then.' He tipped his hat, opened the door and stepped out into the cool, breezy dawn light. He headed for the barn, never looking back but sensing she was watching him from the window.

It felt good to be back on his feet.

It felt even better now that he knew what he had to do.

And as he reached the barn and pulled the heavy

door aside, the smell of horses and warm hay felt strangely comforting and he realized that he'd ruined a good night's sleep ... because, as always, just by letting his thoughts marinate, the decision had been decided for him.

CHAPTER FOUR

It was mid-morning, without the smell of rain in the dry, brittle wind, and already hot when Lawless rode into Santa Rosa.

Originally a small, sleepy pueblo inhabited by Mexicans and border riff-raff, the decision in the late 1880s by the Southern Pacific Railroad to build a station there, which was soon followed by a Harvey House, put the village on the map.

Almost overnight Santa Rosa became a thriving town. Settlers flowed in, eager to become farmers, ranchers or businessmen. Streets were mapped out and lined with stores, cantinas, restaurants, offices, schools and churches.

The need for beef escalated, bringing cattlemen and their herds into the area. Stockyards were built alongside the tracks, and the people quickly elected a mayor, town council and a sheriff to keep the unruly, drunken cowhands in line.

They also accepted Stillman J. Stadtlander's offer to pay for a town hall and a sheriff's office with a jail

36

to hold the disorderly cowboys. They did this despite knowing that by taking his money they inevitably paved the way for the arrogant, power-hungry cattleman to have a voice in every other aspect of the fast-growing town.

And they lived to regret it.

Now, as Lawless reined up outside the sheriff's office, he saw a familiar golden sorrel, with a new bridle and saddle, tied to the hitch-rail. Fate's lack of subtleness almost made him laugh. Dismounting, he drew his Colt, spun the cylinder so that a cartridge was positioned under the hammer and returned the gun to its holster. Then, pulling his rifle from its boot, he levered in a round and entered the office.

Inside, Sheriff Hansen and Latigo Rawlins stopped their heated discussion to look at him. A third man, a tall, skinny deputy named Luke Otis, stood holding a double-barrel shotgun on the small, smartly dressed Texas gunman. He tensed as he recognized Lawless and nervously increased the pressure of his trigger finger.

'Now then, Luke,' the sheriff said gently, 'let's not go off half-cocked.' To Lawless, he added: 'Same goes for you.'

'Don't raise a sweat over me,' Lawless replied, eyes never leaving Latigo. 'I'm just here to thank a friend of mine for savin' my life.'

'Saving your—?' Sheriff Hansen looked confused. 'Ain't that puttin' the truth a mite ass-backwards?'

'Not at all,' said Lawless. 'From what Miss Ketchum tells me, it was Lefty, here, who told her riders where I was lyin' in the dirt. Ain't that so, *amigo?*'

Latigo grinned boyishly and in a soft Texas drawl said: 'Reckon you would've done the same for me.'

'Can the sarcasm, both of you,' Sheriff Hansen said irritably. 'I don't know what the hell's goin' on, but I'm giving you fair warning: either of you try to jerk your iron and Luke, here, is goin' to bust a hole right through you. We clear on that?'

Latigo chuckled. 'Friendly soul, ain't he?' he said to Lawless.

'Full of sympathy an' human kindness.'

'Save your sarcasm for someone who appreciates it,' the sheriff snapped. 'As for you, Lawless, whatever you came in here for, say it and then get the hell out.'

'Be happy to, Will.' Lawless kept his gun-hand near his Colt, ready to draw the instant he sensed that Latigo might try to shoot him – though in his heart he knew he couldn't outdraw the little bounty hunter, no matter how hard he tried.

'What I'm here for,' he continued, 'is to find out what you intend to do about Old Man Stadtlander's men harassin' Miss Ketchum's cattle.'

'Miss Ketchum?' Sheriff Hansen looked surprised. 'Since when'd you become a voice in her troubles?'

'Minute I heard you were ignorin' her, Will.'

'I ain't been ignoring her. But until I catch Mr Stadtlander or his men in the act of buffaloing her cattle, there's nothin' I *can* do. Not legally, and it's got to be legal.'

'That's all I wanted to hear,' Lawless said and

started for the door.

'Hope you ain't figurin' on paying Mr Stadtlander a visit.'

'Where I go is my business, Will.'

'And it's my business to keep the peace.'

'So keep it.'

'Wait up,' Latigo said as Lawless opened the door. 'Mind if I ride along with you?'

'Suit yourself,' Lawless said. He left.

Latigo started to follow him, but Sheriff Hansen blocked his path. 'Hold it. That man's plenty of trouble by his lonesome without you throwin' in with him.'

'Reckon that's my call, Will.'

'I'm makin' it mine, Latigo.'

The color drained from the gunman's boyishly handsome face. 'Sheriff, you know better than to push me.'

'An' you know better than to buck the law.'

'For the last time, Will, get out of my way.'

The sheriff stood firm. 'What I said earlier still stands: I give Luke the word, and he'll spatter the door with your guts.'

'Not before I put a hole between your eyes.' Latigo didn't seem to move yet almost magically his Colt .44 appeared in his hand.

The deputy nervously licked his lips. 'What you want me to do, Sheriff?'

'He wants you to lower that scattergun,' Latigo said. 'Ain't that right, Will?'

The sheriff chewed his lip for a moment, then

said: 'Do like he says, Luke.'

The deputy quickly obeyed.

Latigo holstered his gun with the same blurring swiftness. 'Be seeing you, Will.' He checked his reflection in the window overlooking Front Street, adjusted his black string tie and made sure his spotless, pearl-gray Stetson was on exactly straight and walked out.

'It ain't natural for a man to draw that fast,' Luke grumbled. 'You think it's natural, Will?'

The sheriff was too angry to answer. 'I'll be in Rosario's, 'case anyone asks,' he said, and stormed out.

'Well, I don't think it's natural,' Luke Otis said, answering himself. 'I don't think it's natural at all.' Returning the shotgun to the gun rack, he sat in the sheriff's chair and put his long legs up on the desk. 'An' I'll be happy to tell that to anyone cares to listen.'

CHAPTER FIVE

Neither Lawless nor Latigo spoke as they rode out of town.

But once they were clear of the outskirts, into the open, sunbaked scrubland, Latigo suddenly reined up, forcing Lawless to do the same.

' 'Fore we go any farther,' he drawled, 'I'd like to know somethin'.'

Lawless waited.

'Did you take Miss Ronnie up on her offer?'

'Offer?'

'To ramrod her outfit. Don't look so surprised,' he added as Lawless' eyebrows arched. 'Surely you ain't naive enough to think you're the first fella she's asked?'

'Never crossed my mind, either way.'

'Sure it didn't.'

'I'm serious,' Lawless said, adding: 'So why didn't you take her up on it?'

' 'Cause I never hire my gun out to a woman, 'specially a woman who's got an axe to grind.'

41

'You don't figure she's got a right to water her cows on her own property?'

'Sure she does – if that's all she was doin'.'

Lawless hooked one leg over his saddle horn, took off his hat, wiped the sweat from the headband and fanned himself for a few moments before putting the hat back on. Then, getting out the fixings, he started rolling a smoke. 'Go ahead,' he said when Latigo didn't continue. 'I'm listenin'.'

Latigo scoffed. 'Your ears may be open but your mind ain't. Right now, *compadre*, you're dead set on helping that filly and nothin' I could say is goin' to change your mind.'

'I *said*, I'm listening.'

'All right. Then chew on this: Stadtlander's pure mean. No one knows that better than me, who's done his dirty work from time to time. But that doesn't mean he ain't got the right to water his cattle in the Lower Snake, same as anybody else.'

'What about her rights?'

'What about 'em?'

'You forgettin' the river runs through her property?'

'No. And I ain't forgettin' this is the worst drought we've had in years, neither. Times like now, not even the law would side with her. Dead cattle don't do anybody any good.'

'Then how come Stadtlander can't see it that way?'

'Meaning?'

' 'Cording to Miss Ronnie, she's more'n willing to let Stadtlander or anyone else water their cattle there

42

– but not if it means her livestock are goin' to die from thirst.'

'What're you talking about? The Lower Snake ain't run dry long as anyone can remember.'

'It's not the river she's worried about – it's havin' her cattle driven off by Stadtlander's men.'

Latigo frowned. 'You takin' her word on this or do you know it to be true?'

'I've heard it from enough mouths to believe it's true.'

Again Latigo frowned. He stood up in the stirrups to stretch his legs and then settled back on to the creaking saddle before saying: 'How about we both go brace Old Man Stadtlander 'bout this – hear his side of it 'fore we decide who's right?'

'On one condition.'

'I tell you why I didn't kill you when I had the chance?'

'So it definitely was you?'

'You know anybody else that good with a rifle?'

'I can name at least two, maybe three. But that's not the question.'

Latigo sighed. 'Don Diego wanted you dead. Paid me to do the job.'

'Now I'm really confused,' Lawless said. 'If you've told me once, you've told me a hundred times – you always do what you're paid to do.'

'True.'

'So what happened? And don't tell me you had a moment of conscience – 'cause we both know you were born without one.'

'True again.'

'So-o?'

'Truth is,' Latigo said, truly puzzled, 'I'm still tryin' to figure out myself why I missed. It ain't natural and it's thrown me for a loop.'

A wind-blown tumbleweed rolled, bouncing, past them, causing their horses to stir skittishly.

Lawless exhaled a lungful of smoke and flicked the butt off into the desert.

'So, where's that leave us, Lefty?'

'Pals, same as always,' Latigo said. ' 'Less, of course, you're anxious to prod it further.' As he spoke he flexed the fingers of his right hand, as if readying to draw.

'Not me,' Lawless said. He unhooked his leg and returned his foot to the stirrup. 'I ain't the prodding kind.' He kicked up the dun and rode on in the direction of Stadtlander's ranch.

Latigo scoffed: 'The hell you ain't,' and spurred his mount after Lawless.

CHAPTER SIX

It was a little more than an hour's ride to the tall, arched, signature gateway that told everyone they were now on Double S land. It took another twenty minutes to climb to the grassy hilltop on which stood the rancher's impressive three-story, stone-and-wood mansion.

Stadtlander, one of the first ranchers to arrive in Santa Rosa, had quickly purchased every available acre surrounding the town and stocked them with cattle. He'd spent his money on little else, content to live with his wife, Agatha, in a modest ranch house at the foot of the hill. His aggressive ways, often backed by threats and shootings, put fear into the other settlers and very few of them stood up to him or his gunmen. His herd increased rapidly, as did his holdings, and within a few years he'd established a cattle empire, becoming rich enough to build his shrine – the mansion atop the hill so he could lord his wealthy presence over everyone.

To all appearances he seemed to have the perfect

life. But in fact it was anything but ideal. Agatha, a pale, delicate Easterner of fine breeding, had never enjoyed her husband's rough-and-tumble, testosterone-filled world. And after giving him a daughter, Elizabeth, and a son, Slade, she grew sickly and died of pneumonia – though the folks in Santa Rosa who knew her well believed she just lost her will to live and withered away.

Stadtlander was distraught. In his own strange way he'd loved his wife and her loss cut him deeply. He tried easing his pain by spoiling his children and when that didn't lessen his grief, he took his frustration and anger out on anyone who stood in his way of becoming the 'Emperor of New Mexico'.

But even after he'd crushed most of the local ranchers, he wasn't a happy man. Personal tragedy seemed to dog him. Elizabeth, always her daddy's favorite, had inherited his forceful nature and ability to get things done and it was a foregone conclusion that she – not her whining, spiteful, hedonistic brother – would be the one to run the ranch when her father stepped aside.

But it wasn't in the cards. While still in her early teens she caught yellow fever and despite the best doctors money could afford . . . soon died. Her death pushed Stadtlander over the top. His last vestige of decency vanished, and he became a bitter, ruthless bully who seemed to thrive on other people's misfortune.

Now, as Lawless and Latigo rode up the steep grassy incline, they were well aware of the kind of man they were about to face. They also were aware of the armed lookouts who patrolled the two ornate balconies encircling the mansion, lookouts authorized to shoot any trespassers that posed a threat.

'Don't make any sudden moves and keep your hands where they can see 'em,' Latigo told Lawless. 'Skunks are just lookin' for an excuse to gun us down.'

On reaching level ground, they rode at a walk between the corrals, water tower and outer buildings surrounding the house. Everywhere, ranch hands were busy with chores. A bunch of them were repairing one of the corral fences. They stopped working to watch Lawless and Latigo ride past. Their looks were sullen and suspicious, and several of them grabbed their gun-belts from the top rail of the fence and buckled them on.

'You get the feelin' they don't trust us?' Latigo said wryly.

'*You* – not me.'

'How you figure that?'

' 'Cause it's *you* they're watchin'.'

Latigo looked and saw that Lawless was right. 'Why the hell wouldn't they trust me?'

'Can't imagine,' Lawless said, 'knowing your sweet, gentle disposition.'

Latigo bristled. 'I never drew on a man first or started a fight in my life.'

'No, you just provoke a fella until he's got no choice but to jerk his iron. *Then* you kill him.'

Latigo's amber-brown eyes flashed angrily. 'Don't

prod me,' he warned. 'I won't take that, Lawless . . . not even from you.' They rode on in silence for a few moments, then he added: 'Men I killed deserved to die anyway.'

'Says who?'

'The man dealin' the cards.'

Lawless looked at him in disbelief. 'Let me get this straight, Lefty. You're sayin' God appointed you judge, jury and executioner?'

'Why else do you think He made me so fast?'

It was so absurd Lawless couldn't think of a suitable reply.

'Anyways, they had a chance to kill me first.'

'Sure – 'bout the same chance a gobbler has against a scattergun.'

'Ain't my fault that everyone's slower than me.'

'I'll make a note to remind God about that.'

'Anyways,' Latigo continued, 'just to make it fair, like I said before, I always let 'em draw first.'

'Not always, *amigo*,' Lawless said, indicating the bandage under his hat.

Latigo scowled. 'That was different. It was the only way I could keep my word to the *patron* and not kill you.'

'Oh, that's right,' Lawless said. 'I forgot. You deliberately missed me.'

'Yeah, and I took a hell of a risk by doing it, so can the sarcasm. Word ever leaks out that I missed who I was aimin' at – for any reason – my days as a hired gun or a bounty hunter are number—' He broke off as he recognized the two men who'd just stepped out of the front door and now stood watching them from the porch, then added: 'Looks like we got us a welcoming committee.'

Lawless eyed the two men sourly. They were as different in every aspect as any father and son could be.

Stillman J. Stadtlander had thick, bristly brown hair, a square, jut-jawed face and a look of perpetual defiance in his sun-squinted eyes. In his sixties, his bulky, powerful body looked out of place atop his bowed, stubby legs. He suffered with gout and arthritis, often needing a cane to help him walk, but was fearless and ruled even the toughest of his men with a clenched fist.

His son, Slade, was tall and cowboy-lean, with his dead mother's fair hair and soft, weak-chinned, thin-lipped face that commanded no respect from anyone. A known bully who relied on his father's reputation to keep him out of jail, he was disliked by everyone in Santa Rosa – especially the whores on Lower Front Street who frequently had to endure his abuse or be forced out of town.

Now, trying to assert himself in front of his father, he stepped forward and glared at Lawless and Latigo. 'What the hell d'you two want?'

Lawless ignored him and spoke to Stadtlander. 'We need to talk.'

' 'Bout what?'

'Be easier if we could step down and talk inside,' Lawless said.

'You stay in that goddamn saddle,' warned Slade, 'or pay the price.'

Latigo laughed mockingly. 'The smaller the rooster, the louder it crows.'

Stung, Slade tensed as if he might do something about the insult.

'Go ahead, sonny,' Latigo urged. 'I ain't shot a lily-livered weasel all week.'

'Mr Stadtlander,' Lawless said, 'less you want your boy killed 'fore your eyes, I'd tell Slade to back off.'

'Better yet,' taunted Latigo, 'send him to bed without his supper.'

Seething, Slade stood there desperately wanting to draw but at the same time knowing that if he so much as twitched, he'd end up on the wrong side of the grass.

His father, knowing the same thing, said: 'Get inside, damn you.'

'But, Pa—'

'Now!' Stadtlander snapped. 'That's an order!'

Shamed, Slade angrily whirled around and slammed indoors.

'We'll talk out here,' Stadtlander told Lawless. Then, to his hands, who'd quietly gathered around Lawless and Latigo: 'Anyone who ain't workin' in ten seconds can collect his wages.'

The men hurried back to their chores.

'You can step down now,' Stadtlander told Lawless and Latigo. Without waiting for a response, the rancher limped to one of the chairs pulled up to a nearby table. As if by an invisible signal, a Chinese houseboy in a white coat emerged from the house and quickly pulled the chair out so his boss could sit.

'Fetch somethin' cool,' Stadtlander barked.

The houseboy hurried back inside.

'Sit,' Stadtlander told Lawless and Latigo. They obeyed and were barely settled when the houseboy returned with a pitcher of lemonade and three glasses.

Stadtlander waited until the houseboy had filled their glasses and returned indoors, then asked Latigo: 'What's your play in this, Lefty?'

'That depends on you, Mr Stadtlander.'

'Ever the opportunist.'

'You should know. I've done your dirty work enough times.'

Stadtlander grunted, then said gruffly to Lawless: 'Reckon you're here to tell me not to water my cattle at the Lower Snake?'

'Only where it runs through Miss Ketchum's property.'

'But that's where the river's closest to where my herd's grazin'.'

'So graze 'em elsewhere. Even in this drought I hear you got water up on your north section.'

'I already got a herd up there.'

'Maybe they'd like company?' Latigo said.

Stadtlander ignored him and spoke directly to Lawless. 'Know how much fat I'd lose off my beef if I was to drive 'em that far? Hell's fire, by then they'd be so skinny there wouldn't be enough to feed the buzzards.'

'That ain't Miss Ketchum's concern, Mr Stadtlander.'

'I could easily *make* it her concern.'

'That a threat?' Lawless asked quietly.

'Call it what you like,' Stadtlander said, adding: 'Right or wrong, I'm watering my cows where water's closest and there ain't a rancher around who wouldn't side with me – not in this drought.'

'I'm not interested in the opinion of other ranchers,' Lawless said. 'Neither is Miss Ketchum. All that matters to her is that you tell your men to quit drivin' her cattle away so yours can drink.'

'Why would I do that for?'

'So they'll die of thirst. With no herd, she'll be forced to sell and then you could buy her spread for next to nothin' – like you've bought most of the other ranches around Santa Rosa.'

'Don't try to deny it,' Latigo told Stadtlander. 'You're railroadin' her and you know it.'

Stadtlander erupted. 'Dammit to hell,' he said, pounding the table so hard the glasses rattled. 'Day was I would've shot you both for talkin' to me like that!'

'Be glad this ain't that day,' Latigo said, hand dropping to his six-gun. ' 'Cause you'd be dead 'fore you cleared leather.'

There was a tense, angry silence as both men locked stares.

'Mr Stadtlander,' Lawless said quietly, 'you're missing the point here. Miss Ketchum isn't tryin' to be unreasonable—'

'If you believe that you're a damn fool,' Stadtlander said, adding: 'And it's you who's missing the point.'

'How's that?'

' 'Cause she's playin' you like a cheap fiddle.' He included Latigo as he continued. 'Don't you realize what's happenin'? Veronica's using you – both of you. Got you hooked with her sob story, hoping you'll kill me before the truth leaks out.'

'An' what truth might that be, Mr Stadtlander?'

'That I have a legal right to water my beef at the river, and she knows it.'

'Got any steak with that sizzle?'

'Her daddy's word.'

'Her father said you could water your beef there?'

'Damn right. Anytime during a drought. We even signed a paper on it.'

'I'd like to see it,' Lawless said.

'It ain't available.'

'Or maybe doesn't exist?'

'It exists. Ask Veronica. Her daddy's lawyer has a copy of it.'

'Not accordin' to her. She says her daddy never signed any such paper and never had a lawyer either.'

'She's lyin' through her teeth. Her daddy an' me, we both signed it and then shook hands on it.'

'Would that be before or *after* you shot him?' inquired Latigo.

Stadtlander ignored his sarcasm. 'That shooting's already a matter of record. Her pa an' me, we got to arguing over some stray cows my men mistakenly put a hot iron on and next thing I knew, he was pointin' his rifle at me. Ask any of my boys. I had no choice but to shoot him.'

'Even if that's true,' Lawless said, 'that don't excuse you for driving off her cattle.'

'Like her old man, she gave me no choice. It's true,' he said as Lawless and Latigo looked dubious. 'First time I brought the herd down to the river, I wasn't looking for trouble. But her crew was hiding there, waitin' for us. Got the drop on my boys and threatened to shoot them *and* any steer that took a drink.'

'I'm slow to call a man a liar,' Lawless said, 'but if I live to be a hundred, I'd be hard-pressed to believe that.'

'Believe what you want,' Stadtlander said. 'It don't alter the truth. And the truth is Veronica started this fight knowin' her daddy and me had a contract, and that the only chance she had of winning was to use my reputation against me.' He planted his walking stick, leaned his weight on it and struggled to his feet. 'Now, I'm all done talkin', so get the hell off my property!'

'Wait,' Lawless said as the rancher started to go inside.

'What – an' listen to more of your hogwash?'

Lawless forced himself to remain calm, saying: 'What if I knew a way to keep the peace between you and Miss Ketchum – and still get both of your herds watered? Would that interest you?'

'Go on,' Stadtlander said, leaning on his stick.

'What if you both agreed to bring your beef to the river on different days? Or every other second day?

54

That way, both herds get watered and nobody steps on anybody else's toes – *or* runs their cattle off.'

'That'll never happen.'

'But if it did,' persisted Lawless, 'would you be willing to abide by it?'

Stadtlander frowned. He saw the sense in the offer but had to fight to replace his innate belligerence with consideration. Finally, grudgingly, he said: 'If you can get Veronica to agree to that, I'll sign on.'

'Fair enough,' Lawless said.

'But I need to know her answer fast,' Stadtlander went on. 'In this goddamn heat I can't keep my cattle away from water for more than a day or two.'

'You'll get it before then,' Lawless promised. 'What's more, I'll ride out here and tell you to your face. Till then, though, there's got to be a truce. Agreed?'

Stadtlander chewed on the idea for a moment before saying: 'You got two days, mister. Forty-eight hours. Not a heartbeat longer. After that, all bets are off an' the shootin' starts.' Opening the front door, he limped inside.

Latigo looked across the table at Lawless. 'Think you can talk her into it?'

'For her sake, I hope so. It's not like she's got a lot of options.'

CHAPTER SEVEN

As the two of them rode down the sunbaked hill from Stadtlander's mansion, Lawless felt a cold uneasiness forming in his belly. He looked at Latigo and noticed he looked uneasy too.

'You thinking what I'm thinking?'

'Slade?'

Lawless nodded. 'In the front door, out the back so his old man wouldn't see him leave. That way, he's got an alibi when it comes time to bushwhack us.'

'He won't be alone, either,' Latigo said. 'Probably got the Iverson brothers with him. Wouldn't be the first time those three misfits dry-gulched somebody.'

'Could always take the long way back to town and avoid Bronco Canyon entirely.'

'In this goddamn heat?'

'It was just a suggestion,' Lawless grumbled. 'No need to bite my head off.'

They rode on. At the foot of the hill the trail ran straight across two miles of sun-scorched scrubland. It then forked, one trail swinging south in a long, gradual curve before finally heading north again toward Santa Rosa, the other leading straight to a rocky, steep-walled canyon filled with brush and oak trees. From the other end of the canyon it was only a short ride into town.

Lawless and Latigo followed the trail to the canyon. But as they neared the entrance, they reined up, drew their Colts and made sure they were fully loaded. They then nodded to each other to show they were ready, and spurred their horses into a gallop.

As they rode toward the entrance, each man rose up in the saddle and swung his outer leg over to the inner side of their galloping horse. There, supported by one foot in the stirrup and one hand clinging to the saddle horn, they hunched down so that not even their heads showed above their saddles.

As they galloped into Bronco Canyon, Lawless and Latigo leaned sideways and, Comanche-style, peered under their horses' necks at the canyon walls.

Gunfire came from the rocks high above them.

Lawless got a blurred glimpse of sunlight reflecting off a rifle barrel and snapped off two quick shots. Despite the jarring speed of the mare, his aim was true. Someone cried out and the rifle slid clattering down over the rocks.

More rifle shots came from the rocks on the opposite canyon wall.

Latigo quickly returned fire from under his horse's neck.

Again someone yelped in pain, then was silent.

Latigo kept shooting. He didn't hit anyone but his bullets were close enough to force the bushwhackers to take cover.

More firing came from Lawless' side of the canyon. He felt his speeding horse lurch and knew it had been hit. But the mare continued on, never breaking stride, and shortly they rounded some boulders that hid them from their attackers.

Swinging back up on to their saddles, Lawless and Latigo reined in their horses and dismounted. Blood ran down from a bullet hole in the mare's rump.

'Doesn't look too bad,' Lawless said after he'd examined the wound. 'If she can make it into town, hopefully the doc can patch her up.'

'What about Slade and the Iversons?' said Latigo.

'We'll catch up with 'em another time.'

'We're just goin' to ride off after they tried to kill us?'

'Don't throw a shoe,' Lawless said grimly. 'They'll keep, the mare won't.' Removing Ernesto's fancy saddle, he hid it behind some rocks. 'Going after those bastards now is a waste of time anyway – they're most likely halfway back to the ranch and we can't take on all of Stadtlander's men.'

Latigo scowled. 'I don't like it, *amigo*. What the hell are folks goin' to say when they hear I ran out on a fight with bushwhackers, for Chris'sake?'

'You ain't runnin' out, Lefty, you're saving the life of my horse – a horse that once belonged to a good friend of mine.'

'Who tried to kill you,' reminded Latigo.

'Yeah,' Lawless said, meaningfully. 'But if I held that against everyone who took a shot at me, hell, I wouldn't have *any* friends. Now would I, Lefty?'

Latigo gave him a sour look. 'Keep rubbin' that in,' he grumbled, 'and next time, *amigo*, I won't have the goodness of heart to miss you.'

Lawless chuckled. 'If I'm relyin' on your heart to keep me alive, Lefty, I'm already good as dead.'

It was almost an hour later when Dr Jason Bayless came hurrying into Gustafson's Livery. Joining Lawless, who was waiting beside a stall containing the wounded mare, the old, silver-haired veterinarian apologized for not getting there sooner. He'd had to deliver a foal out at the Ambrose spread, he explained, and had only just run into Latigo.

'Now,' he said, moving beside the bloodstained mare, 'let's have a look at her.' He quickly examined the wound, then took a large pair of tweezers from his bag, sterilized them with whiskey from a flask kept in his vest, and began probing around for the bullet.

The weakened mare flinched and snorted painfully, tossing her head and fighting the rope halter that was tied to the wall.

'Hold her still,' the vet told Lawless. 'The bullet's in pretty deep and I need to get it out before she loses any more blood.'

Lawless grabbed the halter and spoke soothingly to the gray-gold mare. She calmed down a little, but continued fidgeting and nickering nervously as the vet probed around for the bullet.

It took several minutes to extract the slug, all the while blood from the wound streaming down the dun's flank, but finally Dr Bayless said, 'Ah-hah! Got you, you miserable little devil,' and triumphantly waved the tweezers at Lawless.

'Lucky it lodged in the fat part of her rump,' he added, eyeing the bloody slug. 'Any place else and she most likely wouldn't be standing here.'

'She's goin' to be OK then, Doc?'

'Sure.' The vet poured whiskey over the wound, making the mare flinch again, and then took a swig himself before offering the flask to Lawless.

Lawless tilted the flask to his lips, the whiskey burning as it went down his throat, and handed the flask back to the vet, saying: 'How long 'fore I can throw a saddle on her again?'

'Three or four days. Depends on how fast she heals and – oh, be sure to keep the wound clean so it doesn't get infected. If that happens, all bets are off.'

'How much I owe you?' Lawless asked as the vet tucked the flask away.

'One dollar. And if you got an extra blanket, wash it real good and throw it over her. It'll help keep the flies off the wound until it scabs over.'

'Thanks, Doc.' Lawless gave the vet a silver dollar and watched as the old man plodded to the door. There, he paused and looked back, saying: 'I got a busy week ahead of me, but if for some reason her wound doesn't heal or gets infected, let me know. Be a damn shame to lose a pure blood like her.'

He stepped out into the hot sunlight, momentarily

hidden by the glare, and then stuck his head back in the door, adding: 'If you ever consider selling her, I'd appreciate it if you told me first.'

'Got my word on it,' Lawless said. 'But it ain't likely.'

'I don't blame you,' Dr Bayless said. 'It's a rare day when you run across one of these Spanish pure-bloods.' He waved goodbye and disappeared out into the glaring sunlight.

Lawless turned back to the mare. 'Looks like you and me are stuck with each other, *mi belleza.*'

There was a faint chuckle behind him. 'It's a sorry day when a fella's so hard up for a woman he has to soft-soap his horse,' someone said in the doorway.

Recognizing the voice Lawless didn't even bother to turn around.

'I ain't soft-soapin' her, you onion-head. *Belleza*'s her name. Means—'

'Beauty, I know,' Latigo said. 'I heard Ernesto calling her it enough times.'

'What're you doin' here, anyway?' Lawless said. 'Figured you'd be makin' dust by now.'

'Shows how little you know about me.'

'I'm always willin' to listen, Lefty.'

'On the way back from the vet's I stopped at the hotel – got us two rooms.'

'You're stickin' around?'

'Dammit, don't sound so surprised. You think I'd leave you to face Slade and his pack of weasels all by your lonesome?'

'So you do think he's goin' to make a play?'

61

'Has to. If he lets us off the hook after tryin' to dry-gulch us, hell, not even the Iversons will stick by him. And Slade don't have the guts to ride by himself.'

Lawless sighed, resigned, knowing that Latigo was right.

'Let's just hope he doesn't persuade his old man and the Double S crew to ride with him,' Latigo continued. 'Then we really got our hands full.'

'I been thinking about that,' Lawless said.

'And?'

'Wondered if it ain't time we rounded up a little help of our own.'

'Like, who?'

'Gabe Moonlight, for starters.'

'Thought he was still holed up in Mexico.'

'Possible. But if the rumor I heard in Sonora is correct, it's also possible he's just a short ride from where we stand.'

'Ingrid Bjorkman's place?' Latigo brightened. 'There's a happy thought.'

'Wouldn't hurt us to ride out there and see,' Lawless said. 'I'm sure Gus will let me use one of those fleabags he's got corralled out back.'

Latigo wasn't listening. 'Drifter,' he muttered, thinking aloud.

'I was figurin' on him, too,' Lawless said. 'Last I heard he was still in El Paso, and if he ain't Macahan will know where he is.'

'It'll only take a wire to the marshal's office to find out.'

'Why don't you send one while I ride over to

Bjorkman's and find out if Gabe snuck across the border to see her?'

'Will do.' Latigo started for the door, then stopped, looked back, saying: 'He's still facing a rope, you know?'

'So?'

'Well, I was just thinkin'. If you were in Gabe's shoes, would you risk a necktie party to help a couple of broken-down no-accounts like us?'

'He ain't helping us. He's helping Ingrid.'

'Ingrid?' Latigo frowned, puzzled. 'How's she fit in this?'

'If we don't stop Slade and his old man from drivin' Miss Ketchum off her land, Ingrid could be next. Accordin' to Gabe, Stadtlander already tried to buy the Bjorkmans out when Sven was alive. If he runs roughshod over Veronica, it stands to reason that Ingrid's next.'

'I'll buy that,' Latigo said, adding: 'OK, you ride out to her place and see if Gabe's there. I'll work on tracking down Drifter.'

CHAPTER EIGHT

The Bjorkman spread was only a short ride west of Santa Rosa, and a few miles north of the Mexican border. It wasn't prime land, and there wasn't much of it – barely enough acres to support a small herd of white-faced Herefords – but it did have a well that never ran dry, not even during droughts. And that made the land priceless.

As Lawless rode across the scorched scrubland on the roan gelding that Lars Gustafson had loaned him, he could just make out the windmill that pumped the water into the well, its tall silhouette blurred by the rippling heat waves on the horizon. Beside it, he knew, stood the cabin, barn and corrals that Sven Larson had built fifteen years ago when he and his wife, Ingrid, had first settled here.

Lawless hadn't known the Bjorkmans then. But as the town grew, attracting more and more people, he'd occasionally stopped at the ranch to water his horse and gradually, over the years, become good friends with them.

The sound of a rider coming up behind him interrupted Lawless' thinking. Turning in the saddle he saw that it was the Bjorkmans' daughter, Raven, astride a piebald mustang. He reined up to wait for her, marveling as he always did at how unlike her parents she was – both in looks and personality.

Darkly tanned by a life outdoors, with her crow-black hair cut mannishly short, and wearing a doeskin shirt, jeans and knee-high Mescalero moccasins, she looked more like a boy than a girl. She was wiry and tall for her age, fiercely independent, and, though only fourteen, knew the land and the habits of the wildlife as well as any Apache. As a result, the townspeople treated her like a feral child.

But it wasn't only her wildness that caught everyone's attention. It was her eyes. Deep-set and almost too large for her small, oval face, they were so dark that even up close it was difficult to distinguish the irises from the pupils.

Now, as she rode up to Lawless, with two dead rabbits hanging from a string over the mustang's neck, he saw something else in her eyes: anger.

'I ain't going back, Mr Lawless, and you can't make me. So you may as well ride on an' act like you never seen me.'

Lawless frowned. 'Take you back where? What're you talkin' about?'

'Home.'

'Why would I want to do that?'

Raven glared at him with her enormous black eyes. 'You can't fool me, Mr Lawless. I know Momma

65

sent you out here to find me, so don't pretend different.'

'I'm not pretendin' anything, girl. So don't go off half-cocked.'

She didn't say anything, but her tight-lipped expression made it clear that she didn't trust him.

'Why would your mother ask me to go bring you home anyway?'

' 'Cause that's what she does sometimes – send someone to look for me.'

'Well, she didn't send me, so rest easy. Truth is I haven't seen your mother in months.' He searched her inquisitive, dirt-smudged face for some kind of clue that might reveal why else her mother might be looking for her, but saw nothing. 'How long has it been since you've seen her, anyway?'

'I don't know. Day before yesterday, maybe longer.'

'Then I reckon it's time you hightailed it home, don't you? I mean, she must be mighty concerned by now.'

'Why? I could survive out here for days – weeks even, if I wanted. Momma knows that.'

'I'm sure she does. But just 'cause you can kill rabbits with a slingshot, doesn't mean she shouldn't worry about you. For all she knows, you might have been thrown by your pony—'

'Fat chance,' Raven scoffed.

'Oh, it can happen,' Lawless said, 'believe me. Happened to me, more'n once. You're ridin' along and your horse gets spooked by a lion or a rattler and

next thing you know, you're lyin' in a gully somewhere with a busted leg, unable to walk or even crawl
. . . ready to become a pile of bleached bones. How
do you think your mother would feel then?'

'Glad, most likely.'

'What the hell makes you say that?'

'You're not supposed to cuss in front of me, you
know.'

'If you weren't so damn frustrating, I wouldn't.'

'You did it again.'

'OK, OK, I'm sorry. Now, tell me what makes you
think your mother would be glad if you died.'

' 'Cause if I was dead, then I wouldn't be in the
way an' Momma could go live in Mexico with Gabe –
Mr Moonlight. That's all she really wants, anyway.'

He studied her for a moment, troubled, then
slowly shook his head.

'That,' he declared, 'is the farthest thing from the
truth an' you know it.'

'Like hell it is!'

'Hey, watch your mouth, young lady, or I'll dust
your pants!'

'Go ahead,' Raven said defiantly. 'Paddle me all
you like. Won't make me lie an' it won't change the
truth. And the truth is, Momma loves Gabe and
wants to be with him, more even than she wanted to
be with Pa, and that's where I come in.'

Lawless remained silent, knowing she'd hadn't finished.

'As long as I'm around Momma will never sell or
leave the ranch. Heard her say so to him, lots of

times. Which means he has to keep riding up here, where he's wanted, to see her. And every time he does that, Momma gets all upset 'cause she's afraid Sheriff Hansen, or the marshal from El Paso, will set a trap for Gabe. Then he'll go back to jail an' Mr Stadtlander will make sure he hangs, even though everybody knows Gabe didn't steal Brandy from him. And when that happens, Momma, like she says, will die all over again.' She stopped to catch her breath, then said: 'Now do you understand why I can't go home?'

'What I understand,' Lawless said after a long pause, 'is that you need to trust me.'

'Why should I? When growed-ups ask you to trust them, what they really mean is, they want you to change your mind and do what they tell you to do, even though it's exactly what you just said you didn't want to do in the first place.'

Convoluted as it sounded, he had to admit she was right.

'Then I'll put it another way,' he said gently. 'I'm on my way right now to talk to your mother and Gabe, if he's there, about somethin' important. And since I don't have time to argue, I'd consider it a real favor if you'd ride with me. How's that sound?'

Raven hesitated, mulling over his words, before saying cautiously: 'If I agree, and I ain't sayin' I will, what's this important thing you want to ask them?'

'That's none of your business,' Lawless said. 'But if you must know, I need Gabe to do me a favor.'

'What kind of favor?'

'Help me do somethin' – and I'm not telling you what that somethin' is, so don't even bother to ask. Now,' he said when she fell silent, 'you goin' to ride with me or not?'

Again she hesitated, this time chewing on her lower lip.

'Well?'

'Oh, good God almighty,' she grumbled, 'if it's that damn important, I'll ride with you.'

'Now who's cussin'?'

'But I ain't promising that I'll stay or nothin'.'

'Not askin' you too.'

'And if you or Gabe or even Momma try to stop me from leaving, I'll just wait till all of you ain't around or lookin' the other way, and then take off.'

'Fair enough.' Before she could change her mind, Lawless lightly tapped the gelding with his spurs and the roan obligingly trotted off toward the ranch.

Raven sighed, mad at herself for letting Lawless change her mind, and then rode after him.

CHAPTER NINE

As they approached the ranch, Lawless could see Ingrid pegging wet laundry to a clothes line strung between the barn and the cabin.

The sight of her made him feel warm inside. For an instant he envied his long-time friend, Gabriel Moonlight, for being loved by a woman as beautiful inside and out as Ingrid. Then his envy was replaced by a sort of brotherly affection for both of them, and he began to steel himself for the quiet anger he knew she'd feel for him once she learned the purpose of his visit.

On hearing horses coming Ingrid turned, a peg still between her teeth, wet shirt hanging by one sleeve from the line, and broke into a relieved smile as she saw Raven riding beside Lawless.

Quickly pinning up the shirt, she waved at them. Then she stepped over the basket of wet clothes and hurried to the gate. Opening it, she stood there waiting for them to ride up.

Though she wore an old blue working shirt,

patched at the elbows, sun-faded jeans and her hair was windblown, she was a woman no man could easily forget. A Norwegian immigrant whose family had originally settled in Minnesota, she was small and slim, with large, cornflower-blue eyes, near-perfect features, a warm, friendly smile and sun-streaked, tawny hair that she kept pulled back in a bun. But it was more than her looks that made her stand out: despite her homespun clothes and lack of lip rouge, she possessed a genteel elegance that seemed mis-placed in this harsh, parched environment. Yet at the same time, the fact that she'd survived, as a widow, for over two years now, was a tribute to her determi-nation not to throw in the towel.

'Hello, Lawless,' she said as he and Raven rode up. 'What a wonderful surprise!'

'For me too,' he said, reining in.

'What brings you out my way?'

'Well, I was hoping Gabe was here—' He broke off as Raven made no attempt to stop or acknowledge her mother, but rode in through the gate to the barn. There, she slid off the mustang's back and led it inside. Moments later the piebald was running loose in the adjoining corral. But of Raven, there was no sign.

Ingrid sighed wearily and seeing the puzzled look on Lawless' lean, weathered face, said: 'That's proba-bly the last we'll see of her for today.'

'I didn't know the barn had a back door.'

'Doesn't. But there's plenty of loose boards she can squeeze through.'

'Want me to go after her?'

'No. Don't bother. . . .' Ingrid shrugged, resigned to her daughter's erratic behavior, and said: 'Could be halfway to the border by now. Or on her way to the Mescalero reservation. With Raven, one never knows.'

Lawless didn't know what to say, so kept quiet.

'Thanks for bringing her back. I know she can look after herself out there, but when she's gone more than a night I still worry myself sick.'

'That's what I told her,' he said, dismounting. 'It's what made her come home, I think.'

'I doubt that,' Ingrid said. 'Right now she's angry at me – angrier than usual, I should say.'

'Why? You two have a fight?'

Ingrid nodded and tucked a strand of hair back into her bun. 'One of the worst we've ever had – and we've had some real woolly ones.'

'She'll get over it,' Lawless said.

Ingrid's expression suggested she didn't think so. 'It was my fault, I'm afraid. I try not to be too affectionate with Gabe when Raven's around – I know it upsets her because of how she felt about her father . . . but unfortunately, this time I didn't see her coming and . . . well, she caught us kissing and . . . just . . . had a fit.' She paused, pained by the memory, then said: 'You know, Lawless, I've done my best to show that I love her, and to make up for the loss of her dad, but – well, there's times – many times, I'm afraid, when I know she actually hates me.'

'I don't believe that for a second.'

'That's because you're not around her very much.

72

If you were and saw how she acts, what she says to me at the slightest provocation, you'd know I was right.'

Lawless shrugged, as if to brush off her words. 'You know how it is with young'uns. They always favor one parent more than the other. It's only natural.'

'I suppose so,' Ingrid said unconvincingly. ''Course, it's doubly worse in our situation because Raven believes she has a real reason to hate me.'

'What reason's that?'

'Sven's death. She still thinks I'm responsible.'

'That's ridiculous. How can you be responsible for a stray bullet from a bunch of drunken yahoos whoopin' it up? Especially when one of those yahoos happens to be Stadtlander's son?'

'It's not the bullet she blames me for,' Ingrid said sadly. 'It's for insisting that Sven take me into town to pick up a dress I ordered from the catalogue. Says if I hadn't pushed him into it, had waited one more day like he wanted, he'd still be. . . .' She didn't finish and her bright-blue eyes moistened.

Lawless stepped close and put his arms around her, his tone gentle and tender as he tried to soothe away her pain.

'Hey,' a voice demanded behind them, 'what the hell do you think you're doin'?'

Lawless and Ingrid broke apart, both turning toward the man who'd just spoken.

'Stealin' your woman,' Lawless said, straight-faced. 'What's it look like?'

'Like you're stealin' my woman. And you,' he said to Ingrid, 'couldn't you have at least had the decency to wait till I was gone?'

'I tried to,' she said, playing along. 'But he's so virile and handsome I couldn't control myself.'

'It's true,' Lawless admitted. 'Poor woman was so smitten by me, she just had to throw herself into my arms.'

Ingrid smiled, already feeling better. 'Can you ever forgive me, Gabe?'

The dark-haired man, whose name was Gabriel Moonlight, ignored her. He was even taller and broader-shouldered than Lawless, more attractive than any man had a right to be, and his wide-set blue eyes were so pale it was uncanny.

Those eyes now studied Ingrid as if sizing her up.

'Know what?' he told Lawless. 'You want her so bad, take her. She's yours.' He turned and walked to the door of the cabin. There he looked back, adding: 'But I warn you, *compadre*. She's more trouble than she's worth.' He entered the cabin, the door closing behind him.

'Romantic bastard, isn't he?' Lawless said to Ingrid.

She laughed, a soft, lilting sound that came from the heart.

'I wouldn't have him any other way,' she said. Rising on tiptoe, she kissed Lawless on the cheek and then hurried to the cabin.

'Tell him he's damn' lucky to have you,' Lawless called after her.

Again she laughed. 'He already knows that,' and entered the cabin.

74

CHAPTER TEN

Lawless stood in the shade of the barn, back leaning against the corral containing the piebald mustang, slowly rolling a smoke. He enjoyed the process almost as much as he enjoyed the taste of tobacco. He'd heard that in most eastern cities smokers were changing from hand-rolls to machine-rolled cigarettes, mainly because it did away with the mess of spilled tobacco and tedium of building a cigarette that offered no uniformity of taste and lasted only a few drags.

But Lawless did not feel that way. In fact, that special minute or so it took to build a smoke was not just satisfying but also relaxing, allowing his mind to wander over the various problems of the day. His senses never relaxed, though, which is why he heard the faint sound of someone tiptoeing up behind him.

'What do you want, Raven?' he said without turning.

'Did you ask Gabe about your favor?' she asked.

'Mr Moonlight to you,' Lawless corrected. 'And no, I didn't. Not yet.'

'Why not?' Raven said, climbing on to the fence beside him. 'Did they lock you out?'

'Of where?'

'The cabin. They lock me out all the time.'

Lawless flared a match, lit his cigarette, pinched out the flame and flicked the match away.

'Why would they do that?'

'So's I won't see 'em kissing and doing grown-up stuff.'

Lawless inhaled and then contentedly spit the smoke out in a thin stream.

'Not that I really care,' Raven added. 'Soon as I'm growed up myself, an' can do what I please when I please, I'll be leaving to start a life of my own.'

'Doin' what, do you know?'

'Uh-uh. But one thing I do know, it'll be in a big city. Not out here in the middle of nowhere. Unlike Momma, I want to make somethin' of myself.'

'Your time will come soon enough.'

'Maybe. But I'll tell you this,' she said darkly. 'No matter how growed up I get or how many young'uns I have, I'll never lock any of 'em out of the house. 'Specially if I'm a widow an' the only fella I can get is a horse thief who can't rub two pesos together.'

'A framed horse thief,' corrected Lawless. 'There's a difference.'

'Not if the law's in the pocket of the man calling you a thief.'

'Good point,' Lawless admitted, more to himself

than Raven. He waited for her to continue. When she didn't, he tried to think of a way to reach her.

'Miss your pa, do you?' he asked after a long pause.

'More'n anything.'

'Gabe isn't tryin' to take his place, you know.'

'He couldn't anyway, even if he tried.'

'But he would like to be your friend.'

'How can he be my friend? He's an outlaw. One day his luck's goin' to run out and they'll hang him. Then Momma's goin' to die some more and be cryin' all the time, like she was after Pa was killed, and I'm goin' to have to put up with some other strange man sniffin' around her.'

Her voice was filled with bitterness and suddenly it dawned on Lawless why Raven was so angry, and wasn't about to let Gabe or any other man her mother was interested in get close to her.

'What if Gabe wasn't an outlaw,' he said. 'Would you still dislike him?'

'But he is an outlaw,' Raven said, dodging the question. 'And one day they will hang him, like Momma says, so what's the point in pretending he ain't?'

' 'Cause things change, girl. People change. Times change. And you have to learn to change with 'em or get left behind.'

She cocked her head, eyeing him like a quizzical bird. 'What's that got to do with Gabe gettin' hanged?'

'Maybe everything. Stadtlander's an old man and

chances are, when he dies all his petty hatreds and lies will die with him—'

' 'Mean Gabe won't be an outlaw no more?'

'Possible. Most folks already suspect that Stadtlander framed Gabe, so I doubt if it'd take much to get a circuit judge to dismiss all the charges against him. Then he'd be free to live here again and maybe even marry your ma.'

Raven thought about that for several moments, face puckered, teeth torturing her lower lip.

'I mean, would that be so bad?'

'Reckon not,' she grudgingly conceded.

'Remember, if your ma's happy, there's less chance of her bein' unhappy with you. That can't be bad, either.'

'Ra-ven!'

They both turned and saw Gabriel beckoning to her from the cabin doorway.

'Your ma wants you.'

Raven jumped down from the fence, took a few steps then stopped and looked back at Lawless.

'You goin' to tell Momma or Gabe what we just talked about?'

' 'Course not. It's just between us.'

Raven studied him for another moment, her big black eyes not revealing what she was thinking, then she spun around and ran to the cabin.

As she passed Gabriel, walking toward Lawless, she said something without stopping. Lawless couldn't hear what she said, but from his friend's surprised look, he was intrigued enough to wonder what it was.

'Wonders never cease,' Gabriel said as he came up. 'She actually said "hyah" to me.'

' 'Mean she hasn't been speakin' to you?'

'Not lately – unless Ingrid orders her to. I swear I can't figure her out. In the beginning, when I was holed up here, gettin' over my wounds, she followed me around like a lost puppy. And for a while after that, too, whenever I rode up from Chihuahua to see her mother, she was real friendly.'

'When'd she change? Do you remember?'

' 'Bout six months ago. Right after I almost got killed by those three bounty hunters—'

'The ones who ambushed you near here?'

Gabriel nodded. 'They somehow found out I was comin' to see Ingrid that night and had me in their sights. Hadn't been for one of 'em gettin' antsy and only winging me with his first shot, I wouldn't be here talkin' to you now. As it was I got two of 'em and the third, he took off like a scared quail.' He paused and shook his head, perplexed. 'I managed to make it to the cabin and Ingrid patched me up. Seems like from then on, Raven changed.'

' 'Mean, she tried to distance herself from you?'

'Exactly. Hell, it was like I had the plague.'

Lawless knew he was right about Raven then. 'Don't give up on her yet, Gabe,' he said. 'I can't promise anythin', but I think her attitude's about to change.'

'You do? Why?'

'Just a hunch.'

'I sure hope you're right.'

'Patience is the way.'

'Thought it was "caution" – caution's the way.'

'Way it looks, you'll need plenty of both.'

'That's OK. I'm willin' to try anything to win her over.'

'That may be your problem.'

'Meanin'?'

'Could be you're tryin' *too* hard.'

'Reckon?'

Lawless shrugged. 'Well, knowin' how Raven hates to be corralled, my guess is you'd be better off keeping your distance and lettin' her come to you.'

'An' if she don't?'

'What have you lost?'

'Nothin', I guess.' Gabriel sighed and studied Lawless with his uncanny, pale-blue eyes. 'Man, it'd sure be nice if you were right.'

'Only one way to find out.'

Gabriel nodded, paused, mind churning, then said: 'I'll try it. Like you say, what have I got to lose? It can't get no worse between us. And if this works, then maybe, just maybe the three of us could go live some place where my face ain't on a Wanted poster.'

'A family man.'

'What?'

'Gabriel Moonlight, a family man,' Lawless said, chuckling. 'Now I've heard everything.'

'You think you're surprised, *amigo*, what about me? Hell, if Ingrid and Raven hadn't saved my life, I'd be bleached bones by now.'

'Serendipity's a mighty fickle creature.'

'Amen.'

For several moments the two friends just stood there, deep in thought.

'Well,' Lawless said then, 'guess I'll be ridin' back to town.'

'Not till you've had supper. Ingrid's expecting you.'

'Tell her thanks. Some other time.'

'And have her cut off my testicles for lettin' you go? Forget it. 'Sides,' Gabriel added, 'you can't ride out of here without saying why you came here in the first place.'

'Wasn't important.'

'I'll be the judge of that. Now spit it out, *pronto*!'

The sun had gone down and it was almost dark by the time the two of them entered the cabin. There were clean plates and silverware on the table, along with a half-eaten loaf of bread and salt and pepper, suggesting someone had eaten before them.

'You already ate?' Gabriel said to Ingrid, who was washing dishes at the sink.

'The meal's called supper, not breakfast,' she said sharply.

'It's my fault we're late,' Lawless said. 'I got to runnin' my mouth and—'

She cut him off. 'Sit, the both of you.'

They meekly obeyed. Ingrid dried her hands on a towel, went to the stove and began dishing out stew into two bowls.

'Rabbit's burned, most likely so are the vegetables,

but at least it isn't cold.'

Gabriel rolled his white-blue eyes at Lawless, warning him that Ingrid was riled.

'Smells great, honey,' he said lamely.

Ignoring him, Ingrid brought the bowls to the table. She set them down before the men, hard enough to let them know she wasn't happy, then returned to the sink and went on washing the dishes.

Lawless and Gabriel started eating.

'Stew's real tasty,' Gabriel said, breaking off a hunk of bread.

'Yeah,' put in Lawless, 'and the rabbit, it's so tender it's fallin' off the bone.'

'That's because it cooked an *hour longer* than I intended,' Ingrid said stiffly. To Gabriel, she added: 'You leaving tonight or in the morning?'

'Who says I'm leavin' at all?'

'Dammit, don't make it worse by playing games with me!'

'Tonight, soon as we finish supper,' Gabriel said. 'Lawless is expecting a showdown with Slade Stadtlander in Santa Rosa.'

'What's that got to do with you?'

'I'm goin' to back his play, like he'd back mine.'

'Very noble, both of you.' Ingrid said. 'Difference is, Gabe, there's a rope waiting for you. A rope *and* a reward for anyone who brings you in. Oh, and in case you've forgotten, that's *dead or alive*.' She turned to Lawless, adding: 'As for you, I'm really disappointed. Do you really think it's worth either of you getting killed just for the sake of shooting it out with Slade and his men?'

'This isn't about swappin' lead,' Lawless said quietly. 'This is about helping Miss Ketchum keep her ranch.'

Ingrid frowned, curious. 'Veronica Ketchum – where's she fit in this?'

Lawless quickly explained. 'I owe her my life,' he concluded, 'and this seems like a good way of repayin' my debt.'

Ingrid paused, fighting her emotions, then threw down the towel and came to the table.

'I don't agree with what you're doing,' she told Lawless, 'but at least I can understand your motive. Also, you don't have anyone depending on you, so if you want to risk your life for some reason, it's your choice and it doesn't really affect anyone but yourself. But you,' she added to Gabriel, 'you have Raven and me to consider. Oh, sure, we'll survive if you die, but you've led me to believe that I and my daughter mean a lot to you—'

'You do,' he insisted. 'You mean everything.'

'Then how can you throw us away so easily – and all for a woman you barely know and don't even trust?'

'Jesus! If you still think this is about Miss Ketchum – or even Stadtlander – then you ain't heard one word Lawless and me said.'

'Oh, I heard all right,' Ingrid said, flaring. 'I just don't understand, that's all.' Before he could respond, she added, 'Ride with God,' and hurried to the bedroom door. There she paused and looked daggers at Lawless.

'Didn't you think he had troubles enough?'

'Don't take it out on him,' Gabriel said quickly. 'He didn't want to tell me. I had to force it out of him.'

'Lucky you,' Ingrid said. She stormed into the bedroom, the door slamming behind her.

Lawless sighed painfully.

'Don't worry,' Gabriel assured him. 'She'll get over it. She always does.'

'No, she's right,' Lawless said. 'I never should've come here.'

'Then I would've been pissed at you,' Gabriel said, 'an' I'm a lot harder to deal with than Ingrid.'

Lawless didn't answer for a moment; then, remembering something, said: 'Why don't you trust Miss Ketchum?'

Gabriel shrugged. 'No reason.'

'Gabe, don't feed me that crap. Now, why don't you trust her?'

'She's inclined to use folks – men, especially.'

'Use them – how?'

'To get whatever it is she wants – land, more cattle, control of the Lower Snake.'

Lawless frowned, surprised and troubled. 'You figure she's usin' me?'

'Never said that, *amigo*.'

'But you're thinkin' it?'

'Never said that either.'

'Goddamit, Gabe, quit dancin' around the truth. We've known each other too long not to talk straight.'

'All right,' Gabriel said. 'The straight of it is, I don't have any goddamn real reason not to trust her – I mean, nothin' I can point to or tell you true. But my gut tells me not to. That straight enough for you?'

Lawless nodded.

'But that don't mean you shouldn't,' Gabriel added. 'I've been wrong 'bout people before an' probably am about Miss Ketchum, too. So don't be judgin' her on my account. OK?'

Again, Lawless nodded. They went on eating in silence.

'You know,' Gabriel said presently, 'I never figured the four of us would ever ride together again.'

'Drifter hasn't agreed to throw in with us yet,' Lawless reminded him.

'It'd take a natural calamity to stop him.' Taking a whiskey flask from his pocket, Gabriel unscrewed the top and poured three fingers into each glass.

'To the four *amigos*,' he toasted.

'And the mornin' train from El Paso,' Lawless said.

'Amen.'

They drank.

'Damn,' Gabriel said. 'I can't wait for this party to get started.'

'Caution's the way,' Lawless said.

'Caution be damned,' Gabriel said. 'We'll charge to the sound of Garry Owen. Hell, Old Man Stadtlander will never know what hit him.'

CHAPTER ELEVEN

By nightfall, rumors that the Stadtlanders and their gunmen might ride into town at any hour had reached the ears of the townspeople and the streets of Santa Rosa were almost empty when Lawless and Gabriel tied up their horses outside the Carlisle Hotel.

Lights showed in the nearby sheriff's office.

'If we were smart,' Gabriel said, dismounting, 'we'd get the drop on the sheriff and his deputy and lock 'em in a cell. That way, they wouldn't be able to back Stadtlander when he rode in with his men.'

'Leave the law out of this,' Lawless said, pulling his Winchester from its saddle boot. 'We got enough to contend with, without adding to the odds.'

'Twenty guns to four?' Gabriel pretended to look offended. 'Sounds like a fair fight to me.'

'I'll be sure to remind you of that, once the shootin' starts. Now, c'mon. Let's go find Latigo.' Together, like two unstoppable forces of nature, they entered the hotel.

The brightly lit, ornately furnished lobby was empty save for a young, limp-wristed, sleepy-eyed desk clerk who was reading a *Police Gazette*. He looked up, smiling waspishly as he saw Lawless approaching; then immediately lost his smile as he recognized Gabriel. Panicking, he started to duck into the office behind him.

'Hold it, sonny,' Lawless barked. 'Before you make yourself scarce, see if I got any messages.'

'Y-Yessir, Mr Lawless. Anything you say, sir. . . .' The desk clerk checked the rows of pigeonholes behind him and then shook his head. 'N-Nothing, sir. No messages at all.'

'How about Mr Rawlins?' Lawless asked. 'He in his room, do you know?'

The desk clerk checked the pigeonhole numbered 212, saw it was empty and turned back to Lawless. 'He should be, sir. Key's not here.'

'Thanks. Then I'll take my key. Oh, and sonny,' Lawless said as the clerk handed him his room key, 'if you want to see the sun come up tomorrow, tell anyone who asks about me that I came in alone. Got that?'

'Alone. You came in alone . . . yessir . . . by yourself. Oh, yes, I've definitely got that. Yes-I-have-sir. Most definitely indeed.' Fearful, he watched as Lawless walked toward the stairs.

Gabriel picked up the *Police Gazette*, scanned the front page with its banner headlines and gory pen-and-ink drawing of New York City policemen dragging pimps and whores from a brothel, and then handed the paper to the fearful clerk.

'Mighty educational,' Gabriel said pleasantly. 'Makes you proud to know that the law's doin' its job.' He started after Lawless, leaving the clerk frozen behind the desk, his soft, feminine face beaded with sweat.

Lawless and Gabriel paused at the top of the stairs and looked in both directions. Satisfied all was clear, they moved along the hallway and stopped outside Room 212.

Lawless knocked and said quietly: 'Lefty, it's me – Lawless.'

They heard floorboards creaking in the room, indicating that Latigo was walking to the door.

'You alone?'

'No. Gabe's with me.'

The door was unlocked. It opened to show Latigo, gun in hand, standing there in his street clothes. He nodded at Gabriel, 'Gabe,' holstered his gun and stepped back so they could enter.

'Did you reach Drifter?' Lawless asked after Latigo had closed the door.

'Yeah, he was in El Paso with Macahan, like we figured. Wired back that he'd be on the mornin' train.

'See,' Gabriel said to Lawless. Then to Latigo: 'I told him that nothin' but a natural calamity would stop Drifter from joinin' us.'

'I figured he'd come, too,' Latigo said. 'But I expected him to at least ask why we wanted him here. But he didn't.'

'The reason ain't important,' Gabriel said.

'The hell it ain't.'

'You ride with someone,' Gabriel insisted, 'just the fact that they ask you should be reason enough.'

'For you maybe,' Latigo said, bristling. 'Me, if I'm goin' to get shot up, I sure as hell want to know why.'

'Will you two quit flappin' your gums,' Lawless grumbled, not wanting Gabriel to provoke the quirky, hot-tempered little gunman any further. 'We got to figure out the best way to brace the Stadtlanders in the morning.'

'In the street. Head on. How else?' Gabriel said.

Latigo rolled his eyes at Lawless. 'Sonofabitch has been readin' too many Ned Buntline stories.'

'That ain't it at all,' Gabriel said. 'I don't need no fool writer to tell me how to deal with gutless sidewinders like Slade Stadtlander or the Iversons.'

'Keep talkin',' Lawless said.

'Way I see it, we gun those three down, the other men will most likely hightail it out of here.'

'Not if Old Man Stadtlander's there to back 'em up,' Latigo said. 'I know that S.O.B. better than either of you. There's no quit in him. He gets a burr up his ass, he'll fight to the last breath – 'specially if Slade's involved. Then he'll be worse than a cornered grizzly.'

'So how do you suggest we play it?' Lawless asked.

'That's easy. Kill the old man first. Put a dozen bullets in him if necessary, but make sure he's dead. That'll take all the fight out of everyone.'

'I agree,' Gabriel said. 'But I still think we should

lock up Hansen and his deputy first 'cause if we don't, sure as thunder follows lightning, they'll side with Stadtlander and then we got to kill them too. And you both know what that means.'

'Macahan?'

'Damned right. And he's one marshal I don't want doggin' my trail.'

' 'Sides,' Latigo said when Lawless didn't answer, 'locking 'em up gets rid of another obstacle.'

'OK,' Lawless said grudgingly. 'But we better time it right. Otherwise, if word leaks out 'bout what we've done before Stadtlander rides in, we're goin' to have the whole goddamn town breathing down our necks.'

CHAPTER TWELVE

Saying goodnight to the sheriff, Deputy Luke Otis stepped out of the office and stood there on the boardwalk surveying Front Street. Though it was still early evening, very few people were about and all the stores were closed with their windows covered by shutters.

It was an unusual sight, and Deputy Otis wondered if it was worth making his nightly patrol of the streets. Even the few cantinas that were still open, both on Front Street and Lower Front Street, lacked their normal boisterous gaiety, the night seeming strangely quiet without the sound of tinkling pianos, loud Mexican music and raucous laughter and shouting that usually could be heard from blocks away.

But if he didn't make his rounds, Otis knew that some busybody would report it to the sheriff, who would then lecture him for days on end about earning his keep and upholding the law – and, worse still, scathingly remind him that the only reason he even had the job was because his wife was the mayor's daughter.

The repercussions wouldn't stop there, either. There were no secrets in Santa Rosa and Otis shuddered at the thought of facing his wife, a homely, spoiled young woman with a pronounced overbite and the disposition of a Gila monster, who would scream at him for ruining the reputation of her father, a man who had stuck his neck out by insisting Otis be hired in the first place!

No, Otis thought, he'd make his rounds and perhaps, if the gods were smiling, Molly Langhorn would be baking late tonight and invite him into the cafe for a wedge of her wild berry and apple pie.

Biting off a plug of Beech-Nut, he tongued the chew-it into his right cheek, rested his rifle on his shoulder and started along the boardwalk. On reaching the alley separating the sheriff's office from Hayley's Boarding House, he paused and peered into the darkness.

For a moment nothing stirred. Then he heard a groan, followed by the noise of someone moving behind some empty cartons piled next to a side door of the boarding house. Curious, Deputy Otis levered a round into the chamber of his Winchester and cautiously entered the alley.

He hadn't taken more than a few steps when someone suddenly stepped out of the darkness and clubbed him from behind. Tiny lights exploded in front of his eyes. Everything went black.

The next thing he remembered were voices swimming in and out of his mind. He dimly realized he was conscious. His head ached but when he tried to touch it he found he couldn't move. Befuddled, he opened his eyes and blinked a few times until he could focus. It was then he realized he was gagged and roped to a chair in the sheriff's office, and that standing before him was Lawless, Gabriel Moonlight and the diminutive Texas bounty hunter, Latigo Rawlins. Lawless held a rifle that was aimed at Sheriff Hansen, who sat at his desk with his hands raised.

'Tie him up and gag him,' he told Gabriel. 'And make damn sure the knots are tight. We don't want any sudden surprises tomorrow morning when we're dealin' with the Stadtlanders.'

'You're just addin' to your problems,' the sheriff warned Lawless. 'If Mr Stadtlander and his boys are riding in in the mornin', like you say, you'd be far better off letting me handle things, legal-like, than forcing a shoot-out.'

'Thanks,' Lawless said grimly, 'but I've seen the way you "handle" Old Man Stadtlander, and somehow I don't see how you lickin' his boots is any benefit to us.'

Stung, Sheriff Hansen started to protest but Gabriel cut off his words by forcing a gag into his mouth, then tying the ends behind the lawman's head.

Latigo, meanwhile, blew out the hurricane lamp, darkening the office.

'What about our horses?' he asked Lawless. 'If we leave 'em tied up out front all night, anyone who sees them is liable to get suspicious an' maybe figure out that we're holed up in here. Then, there goes our surprise.'

'Lars would most likely stable them for us,' Lawless said.

'If he's got room,' agreed Gabriel.

'If he hasn't,' Lawless said, 'then I'm sure he'll let us turn them loose in one of his corrals in back of the livery.'

'Yeah, but I don't like the idea of gettin' him involved,' Gabriel said. 'He has to go on doin' business here after this is over. And I like that old Swede too much to get him mixed up in our troubles.'

'Why not tie them up in the alley out back?' suggested Latigo. 'Ain't likely anyone's goin' to be nosing around there at this time of night.'

Lawless nodded in agreement. 'Do it,' he said. 'Gabe and I'll hog-tie these two and then we can wait here until sun up. Then we'll head on down to the station and meet Drifter.'

Latigo gave a wolfish smile. 'Be like old times, *amigos*.' He went to the door and paused there to enjoy the moment. 'Sure hope the Stadtlanders don't disappoint us by not showin' up.'

'No fear of that,' Lawless said. 'Old Man Stadtlander's had a hard-on for us – well, certainly for Gabe an' me – for as long as I can remember. He ain't about to let this opportunity slip away.'

'Maybe not,' said Gabriel. 'But I wouldn't count on him bein' surprised to see us. Someone's bound to wonder where Deputy Otis or the sheriff is if they don't show up all night, and come down here lookin' for them.'

'Not much chance of that,' Lawless said. 'Otis

rents a room in Mrs. Conroy's boardin' house and Hansen's a widow with no young'uns.' Turning to Latigo, he added: 'Don't get trigger-happy if you run into anybody. Keep your iron leathered until you're forced not to. Someone hears shootin' and they'll come a-runnin' . . . and the last thing we want right now is to draw attention to ourselves. And before you ask me "Who made you leader?" ' Lawless added as Latigo started to bristle, 'nobody did and I wouldn't agree to it even if you or Gabe did. But someone has to take the point on this, and so far I ain't heard any volunteers.'

Latigo's strange, amber-colored eyes narrowed dangerously, and for a moment Lawless thought the handsome Texas gunman might challenge him.

Gabriel must have thought the same thing because he leaned against the wall, drew his Colt .45 and casually spun the cylinder.

Latigo smiled thinly, but there was no doubt that he got the message. 'Just like old times,' he said softly. Turning, he walked out.

Gabriel holstered his Colt and frowned at Lawless. 'Is it me, or has Lefty gotten meaner?'

'Not meaner,' Lawless said. 'He's just enjoyin' himself more.'

'How can you *enjoy* killin' folks – even if they deserve it?'

Lawless shrugged. 'God knows. Reckon that's what makes Lefty different than us.'

The night dragged slowly but uneventfully by.

In the morning, while the sun was still hiding

behind the mountains to the east, Gabriel remained in the sheriff's office guarding the prisoners while Lawless and Latigo saddled up and rode to the station.

There, according to the station master, who doubled as the telegrapher, the morning train from El Paso was running six minutes late. He examined his big shiny fob watch for the umpteenth time and nodded, as if agreeing with himself.

'Yessir,' he said, closing the lid and tucking the watch back into his vest. 'Six minutes on the dot. 'Least, that's the latest time I got from Red Hill as she roared on through.'

'We'll take your word for it,' Lawless said, smiling at the white-haired, mustachioed, pot-bellied man whose dark-blue uniform looked two sizes too small for him. 'But if you hear anything different, let me know, Cyrus.'

He stepped out of the small, yellow-and-brown station house and joined Latigo, who stood in the shade of the sloping roof overhang. The dapperly dressed bounty hunter was looking eastward along the sun-whitened tracks, eyes squinted as he searched for smoke on the horizon.

'Any sign yet?'

Latigo shook his head. 'No sign of the Stadtlanders, either.' He held his field glasses to his eyes, trained them on Front Street, played with the focus and then grunted with frustration. 'What the hell's keeping 'em?'

'Whatever it is,' Lawless said, 'let's hope it stalls

them long enough for Drifter to get here. Don't give me that look,' he added. 'Unlike you, Lefty, I ain't drooling over the thought of swappin' lead with the Stadtlanders or their men.'

'Maybe you're forgettin' how Slade and the Iversons tried to dry-gulch us yesterday,' Latigo reminded sourly.

'No more than I've forgotten that you took money from Don Diego to kill me,' Lawless said.

'If I hadn't, somebody else would have. And they wouldn't have deliberately missed you.'

Before Lawless could respond, a distant train whistle made them swing around and look toward the east. A smudge of black smoke spiraled up through the shimmering heat waves, making them smile with relief.

'Just like old times,' Latigo murmured. Then, as if he'd just remembered it: 'Know what Gabe told me last night while you were takin' a piss – that if he came out of this showdown still breathin', he's goin' to ask Ingrid to marry him.'

'Serious?'

'Serious as it gets.'

'Then as a favor to Ingrid,' Lawless said drily, 'if Gabe's still standing when the smoke clears, I'll be sure to put a hole through him myself.'

Chuckling, they both stepped forward to the edge of the plank-style platform, eager to greet Drifter as he got off the train.

CHAPTER THIRTEEN

No one in Santa Rosa could remember who first called Quint Longley, Drifter.

Not even his daughter, Emily, or the Mercer family who'd raised her as one of their own.

And Drifter never said.

Not that it mattered. The nickname described Drifter perfectly. For as long as anyone had known him, he'd come and gone as mysteriously as a dust devil, never talking about himself and leaving nothing behind but vague memories.

Only after marauding Comancheros murdered the Mercers and Emily had left St Marks, a convent in Las Cruces, to bury them and sell their property – only then had Drifter finally stopped drifting and bought a small spread outside of El Paso. There, he and Emily began raising horses.

Now, as he stepped from the train into the early sunlight, he shaded his eyes and looked around for the three men he'd ridden with since his late teens. A tall, slab-shouldered man with shaggy dark hair, hawkish features and fearless gray eyes, he didn't see them right away. Then as they approached from the shade of the station house, he realized there was just two of them and he immediately wondered where Gabriel Moonlight was.

'Where's Mesquite?' he asked, using Gabriel's outlaw name. 'Couldn't he make it?'

'He's here,' replied Lawless. 'Waitin' for us in the sheriff's office.'

'Jesus,' Drifter said. 'Is that why you hauled my bony ass all the way from El Paso – to help break Mesquite out of jail?'

'Gabe ain't the one in jail,' Latigo said, and chuckled.

'We'll explain everything after you unload your horse,' Lawless said. 'Right now we're kind of pressed for time.'

With the townspeople staying indoors until they knew for sure if Stadtlander and his men were riding in for a shoot-out, Santa Rosa resembled a ghost town.

As Lawless, Latigo and Drifter rode along Front Street toward the sheriff's office, they caught glimpses of frightened faces peering out at them from behind shutters and drawn curtains.

'Wish I'd known what this was all about,' Drifter grumbled. 'I would've brung Macahan with me. The marshal's 'bout the only *hombre* I know who could make Old Man Stadtlander back down from a fight.'

'Who says we want the bastard to back down?' Latigo said. 'So long as he's alive, Gabriel has to stay holed up in Mexico and every law officer in the territory is itchin' to string him up.'

99

'He could always move away,' Lawless put in. 'I'll bet that Ingrid would be happy to pick up stakes and move to, say, California or even Oregon.'

'All that would do,' said Latigo, 'is stall the inevitable. Somewhere, someday, some bounty hunter is goin' to recognize him and bring him back here draped over a saddle with a bullet in his back. That what you want?'

It was a dumb question and Lawless ignored Latigo. Turning to Drifter, he said: 'I'd like nothin' better than to have this day pass without bloodshed. But we're past that now. With or without his old man backin' him, Slade is goin' to ride in here with a bunch of Double S gunslingers and make sure we're face-down in the street before ridin' out again. And if that don't suit you, *amigo*, or you're worried about not bein' around for your daughter, I reckon you should get back on the next train for El Paso and none of us will blame you.'

'You wouldn't have to,' Drifter replied. 'I'd be busy blamin' myself. 'Sides, a while back Emily and me had a run-in with Stillman J. Stadtlander over her stallion, Brandy, and seein' him humbled, or even feet up, wouldn't bother me in the least.'

'Fair enough,' Lawless said. And that was the end of it.

None of them spoke again until they reined in outside the sheriff's office, dismounted and tied up their horses. Then Lawless banged on the door and told Gabriel to open up.

The door opened almost immediately and

Gabriel, rifle in hand, beckoned for them to come in.

'Everything quiet?' Lawless asked after Gabriel and Drifter had warmly greeted each other.

'So far,' Gabriel said. He thumbed at the coffee pot on the pot-belly stove in the corner. 'Fresh made an' strong enough to boil the rust off your teeth.'

'Sleepy as I am, it's worth the risk,' said Drifter. Yawning, he grabbed one of the mugs hanging from a wall hook, blew the dust out of it and filled it with hot black coffee. As he did he eyed Sheriff Hansen and Deputy Otis, who were sitting on the floor, backs to the wall, still roped and gagged.

'That's a mean way to treat a fella,' he said, blowing on his coffee after the first sip had scalded his mouth. 'Can't we take their word for it that they won't interfere if Stadtlander does ride in, and cut 'em loose?'

'Better yet, why don't I just shoot 'em?' Latigo said. 'Save everyone all around a lot of trouble.'

'I'd like to oblige,' Lawless said, ignoring Latigo. 'But the sheriff's a Stadtlander man. Couldn't trust him no matter what he said. But I'd be willin' to swap rope for leg-irons and wrist-irons.' he added, looking at Sheriff Hansen. 'That's if you got any?'

The sheriff nodded vigorously and said something that was stifled by his gag.

'What?' Lawless said.

'Says they're in the drawer,' said Gabriel. 'Middle one.'

Lawless went to the desk and took two pairs of ankle- and wrist-irons from the middle drawer and turned to Latigo, saying: 'Make the swap.'

Latigo obeyed. When he'd cut the lawmen loose, Lawless tossed him a set of irons. He kept his rifle trained on Sheriff Hansen and his deputy while Latigo shackled them.

'If you two are smart,' he warned, 'when we go out there and brace Stadtlander and his men, you won't make any fuss. 'Cause if you do, I swear I'll turn Lefty loose on you. ¿*Comprende?*'

The sheriff and Deputy Otis nodded fearfully.

'Maybe one of us should ride to the edge of town and keep an eye out?' Gabriel suggested. 'That way, we won't be caught nappin' when they ride in.'

'I'll go,' Latigo offered. 'Bein' cooped up in here's driving me *loco*.'

'Go ahead,' Lawless said. 'But no shooting. Soon as you see 'em, get back here on the double. I don't want Slade or his old man to know we're expectin' them.'

Latigo nodded, grabbed his rifle and hurried out the back door. Moments later they heard him ride off.

Drifter looked at Lawless and Gabriel and shook his head. 'Same ol' Lefty. Never had a lick of patience in him.'

'If anythin',' Gabriel chimed in, 'he's gotten worse.'

'If that's possible,' Lawless said. 'Me, I'm just glad he's with us, not against us.' He went to the gun rack, unlocked it and took down a 12-gauge shotgun. From the drawer below he got a box of shells, spilled them on the desk and filled his pockets. He then took out two boxes of .45 cartridges and opened them. 'Help yourselves,' he told the others. 'Don't want to get caught empty once the shootin' starts.'

As Gabriel and Drifter pocketed extra shells, Lawless moved to the window facing Front Street. Through the sun-warmed glass he could see Latigo riding toward the outskirts. Then the little Texan disappeared around the corner of the church, and Lawless turned back to the others.

He was just in time to see Gabriel and Drifter carrying the sheriff's desk over to the shackled lawmen. Puzzled, he kept silent and watched as they set the desk down between the sheriff and his deputy so that it now separated them.

'What in Sam hell you doin'?' he asked.

'Watch,' said Drifter. He unbuckled the sheriff's belt, while Gabriel did the same to Deputy Otis. They then looped the belts over the chain holding the leg-irons together of each lawman, pulled it through the buckle so that it couldn't be removed and then Drifter tied the belts together.

'Now they can't go anywhere when we go out to greet Stadtlander and his boys,' Drifter said. 'Smart, huh?'

'Now, don't go makin' out like it was your brains that come up with the idea,' grumbled Gabriel. Then to Lawless: 'I saw Sheriff Matt Buckram over in Deming do the same thing once, only he used a stove.'

'He lifted a stove all by himself?' Drifter said.

'No, I helped him,' said Gabriel.

'What were you doin' in Sheriff Buckram's office?' Lawless asked.

'What's that got to do with anythin'?' Gabriel said irritably.

'Nothin',' Lawless replied. 'Just wonderin' is all. No need to get salty.'

'I ain't gettin' salty. Just tired of answering all your damn questions.' He grabbed his rifle and walked to the door, adding: 'I'll be outside.'

He opened the door and left.

Lawless shot Drifter a puzzled look. 'Any idea what's eatin' him?'

Drifter hesitated, as if not sure if he should reveal a confidence, then said: 'Long story. But the short of it is Gabe once found himself a real pretty Mex gal who tended bar in her old man's cantina in Deming—'

'Meanwhile he was playin' house with Ingrid Bjorkman?'

Drifter shrugged. 'Even a good man gets the urge to chase the rabbit now and then.'

Lawless frowned, surprised, but didn't say anything.

'Only lasted a few days an' then Gabe realized what he had, and what he might lose if he didn't rein himself in, and rode back across the border. Last time, far as I know, he ever strayed.'

Still puzzled, Lawless said: 'That still don't tell me what Sheriff Buckram had to do with it?'

Drifter chuckled. 'The Mex gal was his wife.'

'And the part about Gabe helpin' him carry the stove – where's that fit in?'

'God almighty,' Drifter exclaimed. 'Gabe's right. You *do* ask a lot of damn questions.' He picked up his Winchester and went to the door, opened it, started to step outside but instead turned and looked at Lawless, saying: 'Buckram caught up with Gabe as he was leavin' Deming, arrested him and took him back to jail. He intended to hang Gabe and collect the reward. But just like Billy the Kid, Gabe somehow got the best of him *and* his deputy, shackled each one of 'em to a leg of the stove and rode back to Mexico.' Before Lawless could ask any more questions, Drifter left, closing the door behind him.

Lawless stared after him and sighed, still not clear on things.

Just then there was a gunshot. Then another. Both came from the direction of the outskirts and were immediately followed by a burst of return gunfire from a dozen or more shooters.

Moments later Lawless heard a horse approaching at full gallop along Front Street. Guessing it was Latigo, he cursed him for not following instructions, then grabbed his shotgun and hurried outside into the bright morning sun.

CHAPTER FOURTEEN

As Lawless joined Drifter on the boardwalk, Latigo came galloping toward them. Reining up, he brought his lathered horse to a dust-raising, sliding stop in front of them.

'They're right on my damn tail!' he exclaimed, dismounting. 'Slade, his old man and a bunch of Double S riders!'

'Yeah, and thanks to you,' Lawless snapped, 'they now know there's a reception waitin' for them!'

'Two of 'em won't,' Latigo said. 'They're chewin' dirt.'

'Well, that should make negotiations with Stadtlander easier.'

'Dry up, both of you,' Drifter said. 'You're worse'n an old married couple.'

'Quint's right,' agreed Gabriel. 'If we're goin' to survive, we got to quit jawin' at each other and pull together.' Before they could respond, he chambered a round into his rifle and stepped out into the sun-baked street.

Drifter followed.

Lawless and Latigo swapped glares for another moment then shrugged, burying their differences, and joined the other two in the middle of the bright, sunlit street.

There they stood, the four of them, weapons ready, eyes fixed on the church some sixty yards ahead. They could hear riders approaching. Their mouths went dry, making it hard to swallow. All around them the hot, windless air crackled with growing tension.

A minute passed. Then around the corner of the church they came, riding in a bunch, twenty grim-faced, tight-lipped Double S men led by Stillman Stadtlander and his son, Slade, Winchesters in hand.

'Lefty,' Lawless said grimly, his gaze never leaving the approaching riders, 'you told me you'd never drawn first. Don't make this a goddamn exception.'

If Latigo heard him, he didn't show it.

'Just keep your iron leathered till I get done talkin' to the old man. Clear?'

Latigo grunted, displeased. 'Just like the old days,' he grumbled. 'Talk, talk, talk.'

Lawless ignored him. Facing front, he stood there, motionless, rifle crooked over his forearm, watching as the riders bore down on him.

Finally, when it seemed they would ride over Lawless, Stadtlander jerked his horse to a stop and held up his hand for the others to do the same. They obeyed.

Stadtlander nudged his horse forward till he was directly in front of Lawless, who never moved. Never even blinked.

'My boy, here,' Stadtlander growled, 'says you killed two of my men. Any truth in that?'

'Could be,' Lawless said calmly. 'Hard to tell the way it happened.'

'Way what happened?'

'Your gutless son and his pals tried to bushwhack us in Bronco Canyon,' Latigo said before Lawless could reply.

'That's a damn lie, Pa,' Slade exclaimed. He rode up alongside his father, adding: 'They jumped us on the trail an' shot Lyle and Baxter 'fore we even knew what was happening.'

'Mr Stadtlander,' Lawless said grimly, 'you've known me and Lefty for a long time. In all those years, I'll admit we ain't exactly liked each other. But I ask you in all honesty. Does that sound like somethin' either of us would do?'

'Tell that to the two other men of mine that *he* shot comin' into town,' Stadtlander said, thumbing at Latigo.

'I'm tellin' it to you,' Lawless said. 'And I'd like your answer.'

'Pa, don't let him talk to you like that,' Slade exclaimed heatedly.

'It's up to you, Mr Stadtlander,' Lawless said. 'I'm just tryin' to avoid a shoot-out.'

Stadtlander hesitated, eyed his son questioningly for a beat, then licked his lips and turned back to Lawless.

'True or not,' he said finally, 'you expect me to stand by while you people gun down my men – for any reason?'

'What I *expect* you to do,' Lawless said quietly, 'is to teach Slade to be a man and to tell the truth . . . 'cause much as I don't cotton to you, Mr Stadtlander, on your worst day in hell you'd never dry-gulch a man or shoot him any way but face-on. Just ain't your style.'

'Damn you,' Slade hissed and jerked his iron.

He hadn't even cleared leather when Latigo drew and fired, once. The bullet knocked Slade's Colt from his hand, making him curse.

Latigo spun his ivory-handled, nickel-plated .44 and lazily returned it to the holster. 'The next one, sonny,' he said softly, 'goes between your eyes.'

Slade froze. Behind him the Double S hands stirred in their saddles, all itching to take Latigo down but none of them possessing a death wish.

Lawless turned to Stadtlander, his voice quiet and firm: 'Either turn around and lead your men out of here or make your play. Your call.'

The veteran rancher eyed Lawless and the three men flanking him, licked his lips and expelled his frustration in a long, resigned sigh.

Slade, sensing his father was about to turn around, cried: 'Pa . . . I swear . . . he and Latigo gunned down Lyle and Baxter in cold blood!'

Stadtlander gave his son a withering, disgusted look. 'If that's true, then how come Latigo didn't gun you down just now, when it was his lawful right?'

' 'C-Cause he knows you and the men would gun him down seconds after he pulled the trigger.'

Latigo's yellow eyes blazed with rage. No one saw him draw but they did see the Colt .44 suddenly appear in his right hand and knew, just as sure as day follows night, that Slade was a dead man.

'Latigo, please. . . .' Stadtlander said quickly. 'There's no need to kill him. We're pullin' out.'

Latigo acted as if he hadn't heard Stadtlander.

The leathery-faced rancher looked pleadingly at Lawless. 'Call him off. Please.'

'Let it go, Lefty,' Lawless told Latigo. 'You got enough notches.'

Then, when Latigo still didn't respond: ' 'Less of course, you need to boost your reputation by killin' a coward and a liar.'

Latigo stood there for another moment, pinning Slade with a yellow, wolfish glare, and then returned his gun to the holster faster than the eye could follow.

'Just like old times,' he said softly and stepped back between Drifter and Gabriel.

Stadtlander heaved a sigh of relief and nodded gratefully to Lawless.

'Get on your horse,' he barked to his son.

'But, Pa—'

'I swear, boy, if you don't mount up, *pronto*, I'll shoot you myself!'

Sullenly, Slade stepped up into his saddle.

'What about Miss Ketchum's cattle?' Lawless said to Stadtlander. 'Can I tell her you won't be driving 'em away from the Lower Snake?'

Stadtlander squinted shrewdly at him. 'Your offer 'bout me sharing the use of the river – it still stand?'

'Got my word on it.'

'I wouldn't be counting on Lawless' word,' a voice said from the boardwalk.

Everyone turned and saw Veronica Ketchum standing outside the law office of Martin Mayberry. Eyes blazing with anger, she added: 'It's *my* river, on *my* land, and I say you can't water your cattle there – ever!'

'Miss Ronnie, be reasonable—' Lawless began.

She cut him off. 'I never gave you permission to speak for me, Lawless. 'Specially when it involved dealing with this lying murderer!'

Stadtlander erupted. 'Goddammit, if you were a man, I'd—' He got no further.

Because that's when Veronica pulled a small .32 pistol from her coat pocket and fired, point-blank, at him.

Stadtlander grunted, clutched his chest, slumped forward over his horse's neck, and slowly slid from the saddle.

'That's for killing my father,' she said, walking toward him. 'And this,' firing again, 'and this,' firing a third time.

Lawless hurled himself at her and both went sprawling. They grappled briefly for her gun, then

111

Lawless jerked it away from her and got to his feet.

Tucking the gun into his belt, he pulled her up, his face full of anger.

'Goddamn little fool! What the hell's the matter with you?'

'Can curse me all you want,' she said, panting. 'I did what I came here to do – that's all that matters to me.'

'If he dies, you'll wish you'd stayed at the ranch,' Lawless said.

Drifter, meanwhile, was on his knees in the dirt, examining Stadtlander's wounds.

'How's he doin'?' Lawless asked.

Drifter shrugged. 'Reckon he'll live.'

'She won't!' Slade cried – and jerking his gun, shot Veronica.

The bullet hit her high in the chest, near her right shoulder. She gasped, buckled at the knees and collapsed.

Instantly, Latigo drew and fired at Slade. He would have killed him but Slade's horse reared as Veronica was shot . . . and took the bullet instead.

The horse squealed, blood spurting from the wound in its head, and crumpled lifelessly to the ground.

Slade was thrown from the saddle. He rolled over, momentarily dazed, and then got to his knees yelling at the Double S riders.

'Shoot 'em! Shoot 'em! Kill the bastards!'

The Double S riders looked at Latigo, Drifter and Gabriel, whose weapons were pointed at them, and decided that Slade wasn't worth dying for. Dropping their rifles, they raised their hands above their heads.

Slade continued to yell at them – until Gabriel stepped close and clipped him on the head with his rifle butt.

Slade collapsed and lay, face-down, on the sun-scorched dirt.

Lawless, meanwhile, kneeled beside Veronica and cradled her head in one arm. Blood reddened her shirt up around her right shoulder.

Barely conscious, she looked at him through lidded eyes, said weakly: 'I'm s-sorry . . . I couldn't help it.'

Lawless nodded, to show he understood, scooped her up in his arms and got to his feet.

Nearby, one of the Double S riders, the foreman, had dismounted and was tending to Stadtlander.

'Morris,' he yelled at a red-headed man, 'go fetch the doctor.'

Morris, hands still held high, looked inquiringly at Lawless.

'Go ahead,' Lawless told him. 'I'm right behind you.' To Drifter and Gabriel he added: 'Keep 'em covered while I'm gone.'

They nodded. Drifter then turned to the Double S riders, saying: 'Can lower your hands now, gents. But keep 'em where we can see them. Oh, yeah,' he added, indicating Slade's inert body, 'an' one of you throw this sack of mule puke over his saddle, and make sure he stays there.'

CHAPTER FIFTEEN

Dr Roy Shaw was leaving his small, single-story clapboard house, half of which served as his office and surgery, when Morris and Lawless, with Veronica now unconscious in his arms, came hurrying up to the front porch.

'I heard the shooting,' he told them, 'and was just coming over to see if I was needed.'

'She's passed out,' Lawless said, looking at Veronica.

'The pain she's in, it's probably a good thing,' Dr Shaw said, seeing her blood stained shirt. 'Bring her inside.'

'Doc,' Morris blurted. 'Mr Stadtlander, he's been shot up awful bad.'

'Then don't just stand there, man! Go fetch him! Hurry!'

'S-Sure thing.' Morris ran off.

Doctor Shaw motioned for Lawless to follow him and entered his house.

There, in the small, brightly lit, ammonia-smelling

surgery, Lawless gently put Veronica on the operating table.

'I'll take it from here,' Dr Shaw said, scrubbing his hands at the sink. 'Go sit in the waiting room.' As soon as Lawless left, the doctor unbuttoned Veronica's shirt. The blood-soaked material was stuck to the wound and he very gently peeled it back. He then cut open her undergarment with scissors and examined the bullet hole. It was more a shoulder wound than a chest wound, and though it was still bad he sighed with relief.

Going to the door, he called out to Lawless.

'I need you to help me,' he explained as Lawless joined him. 'My nurse is sick and I sent her home.'

'Tell me what you want me to do, Doc.'

'First, roll up your sleeves and scrub your hands clean. And I mean really clean. There's soap and disinfectant on the sink over there.' He pointed.

Later, after the bullet had been removed and the wound cleansed and bandaged, Lawless carried Veronica into a small, unused bedroom at the rear of the house. There, he placed her on the bed and pulled the covers up around her chin.

She was barely conscious. But she managed to open her eyes briefly and smiled as she recognized Lawless. She tried to speak, but no sound came out.

'Go to sleep,' he whispered. 'We'll talk later.'

She mouthed, 'Don't go,' and he shook his head reassuringly. He then unbuckled his gun-belt, hung it over the bedpost and sat in a chair near the bed.

Veronica weakly turned to look at him, and he repeated firmly: 'Go. To. Sleep.'

She nodded imperceptibly, closed her eyes and almost at once drifted off.

About to lean his head back and get comfortable, Lawless snapped erect as he heard the Double S riders approaching. He heard their horses stop and the riders dismount. Then he heard the clomping of their boots as they climbed on to the porch and entered the house. He listened intently, trying to identify voices, and heard Slade telling the doctor that his father was still alive.

Grateful for Veronica's sake, Lawless went to the door, opened it a crack and peered out. He was in time to see Slade, Morris and several other men carrying Stadtlander into surgery. Though still breathing, the tough old rancher wasn't moving and his shirt and jacket were black with blood.

Closing the door, Lawless wedged a chair under the handle, then went and stood by Veronica. She was still sleeping. Even in repose she reminded him of sunshine. On impulse, he bent over and gently kissed her on the forehead. She had something on behind her ears that smelled pleasantly sweet, like fresh-cut hay.

He straightened up, surprised by the fact that he'd kissed her, then shrugged off his feelings and sat beside the bed. He watched her for a while, trying to figure out why she meant anything to him. He didn't remember closing his eyes but the next thing he remembered was someone pounding on the bedroom door.

Instantly awake, he rose, grabbed his Colt and moved to the door. 'Yeah?'

'It's Sheriff Hansen. Open up!'

'What do you want?'

'I said – open up!' Then, when Lawless didn't obey: 'If you don't, I'll break the damn door down.'

'Please, Lawless, do as he says.'

Recognizing Dr Shaw's voice, Lawless reluctantly removed the chair from under the handle and opened the door.

Sheriff Hansen and Deputy Otis stood in the hallway. Both carried shotguns and looked grim. Beside them stood an equally grim Dr Shaw and Slade – though Lawless caught a sense of gloating satisfaction in Slade's eyes and wondered what caused it. Behind them, squeezed into the narrow hallway, were Drifter, Gabriel and Latigo, their tight-lipped expressions warning Lawless that all was not well.

'Step aside,' the sheriff ordered.

Lawless didn't move. 'Not till you tell me what the hell's goin' on.'

'I've come for Miss Ketchum.'

'She can't be moved,' said Lawless. 'Tell him, Doc.'

'He ain't here to move her,' Slade said smugly. 'He's arrestin' her.'

'For what?'

'Attempted murder,' Sheriff Hansen said.

'You must be *loco*,' Lawless said. 'That charge will never stick. Fact is, way most folks 'round here feel about Stadtlander, she'll probably get a medal.'

117

'Wouldn't say that if it was your pa she tried to kill,' Slade said angrily.

'You'd string her up in a second.'

Lawless lost it. 'Will, get that yellow-spined sonofabitch out of here 'fore I kill him.'

There was such boiling venom in his voice that Sheriff Hansen quickly nodded to the Double S riders, who dragged Slade from the room. Lawless could hear him loudly protesting in the hallway, his shouting mingled with the calming tones of his men as they half-carried, half-pulled him outside.

Lawless then grudgingly stepped back, allowing the sheriff, his deputy and Dr Shaw to enter.

'How long before Miss Ketchum can be moved?' Sheriff Hansen asked.

Dr Shaw shrugged. 'Two or three days. Depends on how fast she recovers.'

Sheriff Hansen turned to his deputy. 'You stay here, Otis, till I can relieve you. Sit right outside the door and don't let nobody 'cept the doc or me in.'

'Sure thing.'

'I'll expect you to give me a daily report,' Sheriff Hansen told Dr Shaw.

'Be happy to, Will.'

The sheriff turned to Lawless: 'Miss Ketchum's in my custody and from now on no one sees her without my permission.'

Lawless looked at Veronica, saw she was still asleep and grudgingly left the room.

CHAPTER SIXTEEN

Outside, Lawless paused on the porch while Gabriel, Latigo and Drifter mounted their horses. Not far from them Slade stood talking to the Double S riders.

'Come on,' Drifter called to Lawless. 'What're you waitin' for?'

'Justice.'

'You'll grow old an' cracked in the head 'fore that happens,' Gabriel began – then stopped as Sheriff Hansen emerged from the house.

Lawless immediately confronted him.

'Get out of my way,' the sheriff ordered.

'Not before you tell me why the hell you didn't arrest Slade, too.'

'For what – tryin' to protect his father from a half-crazed woman with a gun—?' He broke off, alarmed, as Lawless drew his Colt and pressed it against his forehead.

'Might want to rethink those words, Will.'

Sheriff Hansen paled and nervously licked his lips.

'Easy,' Gabriel said gently to Lawless. 'Don't lose your head, *amigo*.'

Lawless ignored him. Keeping his six-gun pressed against the sheriff's forehead, he said grimly: 'I'm waitin', Will.'

Sweat beaded on the lawman's forehead. He gulped and said hoarsely: 'What else do you call someone who shoots an old man for no reason?'

'Miss Ketchum had a reason,' Lawless said. 'A damned good one. Stadtlander gunned down her pa for tryin' to defend his water rights.'

'That's a lie!' Slade blurted. 'They was talkin' and suddenly Mr Ketchum got angry over something 'bout a contract and tried to shoot my father. I was there. Saw it with my own eyes. He gave Daddy no choice.'

'Circuit judge saw it the same way,' Sheriff Hansen rasped. 'He cleared Mr Stadtlander of all charges. Miss Ketchum knew that. She was there when the judge made his decision.'

'An' *I* was there, in the street,' Lawless said angrily, 'when Slade put a bullet in her – and that was *after* she shot Stadtlander and *after* I knocked her down and took the gun from her. It was done out of pure orneriness.'

'If that's true,' Sheriff Hansen said, 'it'll come out at her trial. Then it's up to a judge to decide what to do about her and Slade. Meanwhile, I'm just doin' my sworn duty by arresting Miss Ketchum—'

'Before you get too righteous an' make Stadtlander out to be a goddamn saint,' Latigo snarled, 'I ramrodded for the old man. Saw how he bullied folks, 'specially the ones who couldn't fight back.'

'Don't matter,' the sheriff said. 'It was all legal.'

'Like hell it was! Take you, for instance. It was my gun, and the guns of others like me, that got you elected.'

'You suggesting the votin' was rigged?'

'I ain't "suggestin" it,' Latigo said, 'I'm stating a fact. To your face. The votin' was rigged else you wouldn't be wearin' that star.'

Stung, Sheriff Hansen said: 'Easy to insult me when your friend's got a .45 against my head.'

'I can fix that,' Lawless said. He holstered his Colt and stepped back, out of Latigo's way. 'He's all yours, Lefty.'

Latigo smiled wolfishly. 'You were sayin', Will?'

Sheriff Hansen froze. He looked about him, saw Slade and the Double S riders watching him expectantly, and stammered: 'Y-You can't provoke me into jerkin' my iron, so save your breath.'

Latigo laughed and spat in disgust. 'I don't need to provoke you, Will. Not to shoot you. Hell, I'd consider it a public service.'

The sheriff stiffened, but kept his hand away from his gun. 'I don't provoke,' he repeated. 'I don't provoke.'

'Forget it,' Drifter told Latigo. 'Ain't worth wastin' lead on a weasel like him.'

Latigo nudged his horse forward until he was almost on top of the sheriff, then said: 'I'm goin' to let you ride out of here, Will. But know this: Stadtlander's no good. He buys whatever he wants an' he wants everything. And that includes people's souls. Take them circuit judges – they're in his pocket same as you. If they weren't, Gabe would still be a free man . . . instead of an outlaw that every tin star in the territory has been tryin' to hang for stealin' a horse he won straight up.'

'I know he won it fairly,' the sheriff said. He tried to swallow but his saliva had dried up. 'That's why I never went after Gabe myself. Not even though I knew he was crossin' the border now and then to hang his hat at the Bjorkman spread. You think I didn't know you was there?' he added to Gabriel. 'Jesus, you couldn't have been more obvious if you'd hung a sign on my office door!'

'I ain't at her spread now,' Gabriel said. 'So why don't you try'n fit me for that rope while everybody's lookin' on? C'mon, Will,' he taunted when the sheriff didn't move, 'make your play.'

'You're wastin' your time, Gabe,' Latigo said mockingly. 'You heard the sheriff – he don't provoke.'

Stung by his sarcasm, Sheriff Hansen knew that everyone was waiting to see how he'd react. But he was too savvy to let himself be drawn into a fight he knew he couldn't win and, keeping his hand away from his gun, he said: 'My business here is done. As for fitting you for a rope, Gabe, it's like I just told you. I know you got a raw deal and I don't intend on huntin' you down today or any other day.' Not waiting for Gabriel to respond, he stepped off the porch and walked with as much dignity as he could muster to his horse.

'Just as I figured,' Gabriel said loud enough for everyone to hear. 'Yellow as summer corn.'

Sheriff Hansen seethed, but ignored the insult. Mounting, he motioned for Slade and the Double S riders to follow him and rode off.

'What're we goin' to do now?' Latigo asked Lawless.

'Well, I don't know 'bout you three, but I intend to stay here and keep an eye on Miss Ronnie till she's well enough to be moved.'

'Then, what?' said Gabriel.

'I'll take her home.'

'Sheriff Hansen might have somethin' to say about that,' Latigo said.

'Yeah,' Drifter agreed. 'An' much as I hate to side with that mealy-mouthed bastard, with all the witnesses who saw her shoot Stadtlander he'd be justified to keep her locked up till the circuit judge arrives.'

'He's got to get her to jail first,' Lawless said grimly. 'And before I'll let that happen, I'll take her 'cross the border. Maybe hole up with you,' he added to Gabriel. 'That's if you don't mind company for a spell.'

'*Mi casa, su casa, amigo.*'

'Or we could shoot Hansen,' Latigo suggested. 'With the sheriff dead, it ain't likely that long drink of piss, Otis, would try to carry out the charges.'

'Count me out,' Drifter said. 'Like I told you

before, I don't shoot lawmen.'

'Me neither,' said Lawless.

Gabriel shrugged. 'Count me out as well. Macahan's always figured I was railroaded by Stadtlander an' never come after me. But he couldn't stand by and let a lawmen get killed – not even a lawman like Sheriff Hansen – without goin' after the shooter. And life's too goddamn short to have Macahan on my tail.'

Latigo scoffed. 'Macahan, Macahan, that's all I hear out of you three. You'd think he was the Grim Reaper to hear you talk!'

'He's as close to it as I ever want to see,' said Gabriel.

'Well, he don't bother me none,' Latigo said. 'Hell, he comes after me an' I'll send him to hell, too.'

Lawless looked at the little Texas bounty hunter and shook his head. 'I don't know why, Lefty, but you never cease to amaze me.'

'Yeah? Why?'

' 'Cause I never can truly believe that a man was born without a conscience.'

'Conscience be damned,' Latigo said. 'Life ain't about conscience, it's about survival. Eat or be eaten. And I don't plan on bein' anybody's Last Supper.'

Lawless absently touched the scab-covered wound above his left ear before saying: 'Strange choice of words, comin' from you, Lefty.'

'I've read the Good Book, same as everybody else,' Latigo said defensively.

'Yeah, but you've only remembered five words from it: An eye for an eye.'

'So what? They suit me. That's all that matters.'

'Maybe so,' Lawless said. 'But I want you to keep this in mind: Ezra's a good friend of mine. And I reckon you two' – he looked at Gabriel and Drifter – 'feel the same way 'bout him. So there'll no shootin' Will Hansen, or any other lawman, and that way we'll keep Ezra out of this. Agreed?'

'Agreed,' Drifter and Gabriel said together.

'Lefty?'

Latigo grudgingly nodded. 'If that's the way you want it. . . .'

'I do,' said Lawless. 'And I know Miss Ronnie would, too.'

'Is that important?' Latigo said. 'How she thinks, I mean?'

'To me it is.'

'You seem mighty taken with her,' Gabriel said.

'I am.'

'Enough to maybe buck the law if necessary?'

Lawless nodded. The others looked surprised.

'She means *that* much to you?' Gabriel said.

'Yep.'

'Since when?'

'I don't know. I been tryin' to figure that out for quite a spell. An' the best I can come up with is somewhere along the way it just happened.'

' 'Be damned,' said Latigo, adding: 'She feel the same 'bout you?'

'I don't know.'

'I do,' Drifter said. 'I seen the way she looks at you. An' it sure as hell ain't the way she looks at us.'

'She's a mite young,' Gabriel cautioned.

'She's old enough to know her own mind,' Lawless said, 'an' that's plenty old enough for me.'

'Might want to give it some more time 'fore you jump in with both feet.'

'Still don't trust her, huh?'

Before Gabriel could reply, Dr Shaw came out on to the porch. 'Lawless.'

'Yeah, Doc?'

'Veronica's asking for you.'

Drifter laughed softly. 'That answer your question?' he asked Lawless.

'Probably just the first name that come to her.'

'Oh, sure,' Gabriel said. He looked at Latigo and both grinned lecherously.

'Cut it out,' Lawless growled at them.

Ignoring him, Latigo turned to Gabriel and in a woman's voice, squealed: 'Oh, you are so-o handsome, Mr Moonlight. I just *lo-ove* you to death.'

'I'm warnin' you,' Lawless threatened. 'Cut it out.'

'An' I *lo-ove* you too, Miss Rawlins,' Gabriel cooed. 'Will you elope an' make babies with me?'

'Go to hell,' Lawless cursed. When they broke out laughing, he grabbed the old wooden rocking chair on the porch and hurled it at them. The chair bounced, twice, and broke into pieces near their horses. Frightened, they whinnied and jumped back, almost unseating their riders.

The three men laughed even harder.

Lawless rolled his eyes at Dr Shaw, who chuckled and said: 'Incorrigible, all of them.'

Lawless shook his head in half-hearted disgust and entered the house.

Sobering, Drifter calmed his horse and asked the doctor how Veronica was doing.

'She just woke up,' Dr Shaw said. 'But she seems to be a little stronger.'

'Strong enough to make it across the border?' Gabriel asked.

'Not unless she wants to tear open her stitches and have the wound start bleeding again,' Dr Shaw said.

'So when *can* she travel, Doc?' Drifter pressed. 'With Sheriff Hansen on the prod, it's real important for her an' Lawless to get out of Santa Rosa.'

Dr Shaw shrugged. 'Day after tomorrow, earliest. And even then she's taking a chance.'

'How 'bout Old Man Stadtlander?' Latigo asked. 'Any risk of him dyin'?'

'There's always that risk,' Dr Shaw said. 'Any man shot three times can count himself real lucky if he lives to talk about it. But, I like his chances.' Before they could ask him any more questions, he entered the house.

'What do you reckon we should do?' Gabriel asked Drifter.

' 'Bout what?'

'Stopping the law from interferin' with Lawless and Miss Ronnie's plans.'

'I been giving that careful thought,' Drifter said. 'An' about the only solution I can think of that don't end badly is to cause a diversion.'

'What kind of diversion?'

'I ain't figured that out yet. So if either of you have got any ideas, don't be bashful 'bout sharing 'em.'

'Don't count on me,' Latigo grumbled. 'If I slapped leather slow as my brain turns over, I would've been feet up a long time ago.'

'Same goes for me,' Gabriel echoed.

'Reckon it's up to me, then,' said Drifter.

CHAPTER SEVENTEEN

Deputy Luke Otis shifted positions for the umpteenth time as he tried to get comfortable on the hard-backed chair that was outside the door of the bedroom containing Veronica. He would have preferred to be sprawled out on the old leather sofa in the parlor, but Dr Shaw hadn't suggested it and, more importantly, Sheriff Hansen had insisted he sit by the door.

It was stifling hot in the hallway that led from the parlor to the bedrooms, and Otis fought not to fall asleep. Yawning, he brushed away a fly that buzzed about his face, only to have it settle on the stock of the Winchester resting across his knees. He watched it crawl toward his hands, both of which rested atop the rifle, and again irritably brushed it away.

That's when he heard footsteps. Looking up, he saw Dr Shaw approaching.

'I ain't heard a peep out of her,' he said, trying to

make it clear that he was guarding the patient. 'Fact is, I was just figurin' on lookin' in on her to make sure she was all right.'

'Thank you, but that's not your job,' Dr Shaw cautioned. He brushed past the tall, lanky deputy and entered the bedroom.

Otis, stung by the doctor's curtness, muttered something about some folks not being grateful for anything, and settled back in the chair.

In the bedroom Dr Shaw found Veronica awake but still pale and weak from loss of blood. Even with the window open, the room was as hot as the hallway. Picking up a towel, he dipped it in a basin of water on the nightstand and used it to wipe the sweat from her face.

'That better, my dear?'

She nodded and smiled wearily.

'Now let's take a look at you,' he said, referring to her wound. 'It may hurt a little, but it's terribly important that we keep the wound clean.'

She nodded again to show she understood.

Gently removing the bandage, he examined her wound. It was still raw and ugly but showed no signs of being infected and the stitches he'd so carefully sewn were holding fine.

With great effort Veronica moved her lips. Not hearing what she said, Dr Shaw leaned over and placed his ear against her mouth.

'Am I . . . going to . . . be all right?' she whispered.

He smiled reassuringly. 'You're going to be fine, my dear. Just fine.' Straightening up, he replaced the bloodstained dressing with a fresh piece of gauze and rewrapped the bandage over it. 'But you need to get lots of rest and sleep, so your body has a chance to heal itself.'

'. . . W-Want . . . to go home,' she said weakly.

'Right now that's out of the question. As I told Lawless, you'll have to stay here for another day or two at least. Then, maybe—'

She cut him off. 'The sheriff. . . ?'

'What about him, my dear?'

'. . . Heard him talking . . . am I really under arrest?'

'I wouldn't worry about that now—'

'So it's true?' she interrupted.

' 'Fraid so. But—'

'Is he alive?'

'Stadtlander, you mean?' At her weak nod, Dr Shaw added: 'Yes. But he's in serious condition and, like you, can't be moved—'

'. . . Wish I'd killed him.'

'Now, now, my dear. You mustn't get all riled up. It's not good for you. 'Sides, you really don't mean that.'

'I mean it with all my heart,' Veronica said bitterly. 'What's more, I'd do it all over again if I could. . . .' Exhausted by her rage, she closed her eyes and drifted off to sleep.

Sighing, Dr Shaw placed his hand on her fore-head. Her flesh felt moist but cool against his palm and satisfied, he quietly left the room.

As the door closed behind the doctor Lawless

appeared at the open window. Seeing no one around, he quietly swung his legs over the sill and climbed inside. He paused, listening intently to see if he'd been heard. When the door didn't open, he moved silently to the bed and looked down at Veronica.

For several moments she remained asleep. Then, as if awakened by his presence, she opened her eyes. Seeing him startled her and he quickly covered her mouth with his hand, muffling her words. Then pressing his finger to his lips to warn her to be quiet, he whispered: 'I can't stay long.'

She nodded to show she understood. 'D-Deputy Otis,' she began.

Lawless stopped her. 'He's sitting outside the door, yes, I know. I was at the window when Sheriff Hansen was with you. In case you don't know,' he added, 'the sheriff's askin' for volunteers to guard Doc's house.'

'But he knows ... I ... I'm too weak to go any-where.'

'This ain't about you, Miss Ronnie. It's me he's after. That's why he wants to keep you here as long as possible – as bait. It's easier to round up volunteers to watch this house than your place way out of town.'

She immediately grew alarmed. 'You must go. Hurry! Before someone sees you.'

'I will.'

'You mustn't come back ... or try to see me. The sheriff will ... arrest you.'

Fear made her raise her voice and though she was still barely speaking above a whisper, he shushed her and listened to see if the deputy had heard her.

Again, no one entered. Leaning close, Lawless said softly: 'Day after tomorrow, if the doc agrees that it's OK to move you, Sheriff Hansen and a bunch of special deputies are takin' you to jail.'

'I know.'

'I ain't goin' to let that happen.'

She panicked. 'N-No, no, you mustn't interfere—'

'Shhh. Don't talk. Just listen. . . .'

'But—'

'Listen, I said.'

She listened. And when Lawless got through explaining his plan, she was even more alarmed than before. But no matter how hard she begged him not to risk his life and try to rescue her, he adamantly refused to change his mind.

He wasn't going to let her go to jail, or prison, and that was all there was to it.

CHAPTER EIGHTEEN

Surprisingly, Lawless didn't visit Veronica during the next two days. Instead, first Latigo and then Drifter came in his place. Though disappointed, once she learned why Lawless wasn't there she understood his reasoning.

'The sheriff's special deputies are watchin' this place day and night,' Latigo explained, 'so they know exactly who's comin' to see you.'

'I know,' Veronica said, 'I've done a lot of looking out the window lately, and seen them patrolling the fences.'

'That's 'cause the sheriff *wants* you to see them, Miss Ronnie – you and everyone else to boot. That way, he figures, no one's goin' to be damn fool enough to try to smuggle you out of here – not even when you're well enough to leave.'

'Dr Shaw wouldn't let me go now anyway,' Veronica grumbled. 'I can't even get out of bed till tomorrow morning, earliest.'

'Does Sheriff Hansen know that?'

'Yes. The two of them were talking outside my door just before you arrived, and I heard the sheriff asking that very same question.'

'What did the doc tell him?'

'Just what I told you. And he was very emphatic about it, too. What's more, he wasn't very encouraging when Sheriff Hansen asked him when I'd be well enough to be transferred to jail. Said he couldn't guarantee when that day would be . . . and that if I was moved prematurely, the sheriff would be responsible if I had a relapse or, worse, died. I knew Dr Shaw was exaggerating, but no one else would've known it – not by the way he was talking.'

'Good,' Latigo said. 'That ought to hold off Hansen for a spell.' He paused, trying to remember exactly what Lawless had asked him to say, then continued. 'Lawless figures if he pretends not to care enough about you to come and see you – not even when you might be goin' to prison soon – the sheriff won't suspect that he's plannin' to rescue you right under his nose.'

Dr Shaw stuck to his word. Veronica wasn't allowed out of bed until the morning of the second day, and only then after he'd given her strict instructions that she was not to leave the house – under any circumstances.'

'Don't worry,' she assured him as they ate breakfast together in his sunny little parlor. 'Though I feel much stronger and steadier now, I wouldn't want to try to walk too far or even attempt to get on a horse.

My goodness me, I'm having enough trouble just trying to eat with one hand. Fortunately,' she added, 'it's my left shoulder. If it'd been my right, you might be spoon-feeding me right now.'

Dr Shaw laughed. 'I'd be happy to, my dear. Just so you promise to do the same for me when I get too old and feeble to feed myself.'

'It's a promise,' Veronica agreed happily. Then as it struck her: 'How's Mr Stadtlander coming along?'

'He'll live. But it'll be a spell before his son can take him back to the ranch.'

Veronica sighed, troubled by her thoughts, and said: 'I suppose I should be sorry for shooting him, but I'm not. He shot my father in cold blood and—' She paused, frowning, as through the curtained parlor window she noticed two of the special deputies talking outside the front gate. They spoke briefly and then continued on their separate ways. Knowing there were other deputies strategically positioned around the doctor's fenced property, it suddenly sank in that she really was a prisoner.

Worse, awaiting her was prison or possibly even a rope. The thought was depressing, even frightening, and for the first time since Lawless' visit, she panicked and decided not to try to dissuade him from attempting to help her escape. Of course, even if she did escape it meant she would become a fugitive, like Gabriel Moonlight, and would probably lose her ranch and have to hide out in Mexico. But anything was better than prison – even the raw, primitive conditions she would face in the wilds of Sonora or

Chihuahua. Besides, no matter where she went she'd have Lawless with her and just the comforting thought of his presence eased her fears.

Dr Shaw's quiet, gentle voice interrupted her thoughts. 'Are you feeling faint, my dear?'

'W-What? Oh, no . . . no, I'm fine, thank you.' She smiled reassuringly at him. 'But you're right about not overdoing things. Soon as I've finished my coffee, I think I'll go back to bed. I'm feeling a bit ragged.'

Lawless sat atop a nearby hill, the sun brutally hot on his back, field glasses to his eyes, watching the special deputies patrolling the perimeter of Dr Shaw's fenced property. They walked in pairs, all carrying rifles as well as handguns, moving back and forth with the precision of military sentries.

A noise behind Lawless made him lower his glasses and turn around. Below, on the rear slope, Latigo and Drifter were dismounting beside Lawless' line-backed dun. Tying their horses to a bush, they grabbed their rifles and started up the slope toward him, zigzagging through the clumps of tree-cholla that covered the sun-bleached hilltop.

'Where's Gabe?' he asked as they sat, sweating, beside him.

'Where do you think?' Latigo replied irritably. 'With *her*.'

Hiding his disappointment, Lawless said: 'Don't throw a shoe, Lefty. He'll be here.'

'He was *supposed* to be here now.'

'I know. But we still got three hours of sunlight.

Gabe'll be here before nightfall, count on it.'

'I wouldn't blame him if he wasn't,' Drifter said, scratching a match on his boot-heel and lighting a smoke. 'Ingrid's one fine-lookin' woman.'

Lawless chuckled. 'Lat doesn't blame him, he's jealous of him. Right, Lefty?'

'That ain't it at all,' Latigo snapped. 'I just can't figure out what she sees in him is all.'

Lawless grinned. ''Mean, other than the fact that Gabe's ten feet tall, has shoulders wider than a barn, and is better lookin' than most stage actors that parade through here from time to time?'

'Bein' tall ain't everything,' Latigo grumbled. He leaned back, using his hat to shade his eyes against the glaring sun as he watched a hawk circling overhead on outstretched wings. 'Hell, lots of gals prefer short over tall.'

'Well, you'd be the one to know,' Lawless said drily.

Latigo ignored the jab. 'I wouldn't want his shoulders, neither. Gabe told me himself, he has to get shirts special made to fit him.'

'That so?' Lawless winked at Drifter, who grinned and exhaled smoke toward the brilliant blue sky. 'Well, when you look at it that way, and add up all his faults, I reckon you're right: Gabe ain't much of a catch at that.'

Drifter chuckled softly, but remained straight-faced.

'On top of that, he's an outlaw,' Latigo reminded them, 'so he'll never be able to settle down with Ingrid an' raise a family.'

'Lefty's got a good point there,' Drifter said, trying not to grin.

'True,' Lawless agreed. 'But the one thing we're all forgettin' is, Ingrid don't give two hoots about any of those things. 'Cording to her, bein' with Gabe part-time is better than bein' with any other man full-time.'

Latigo grunted, displeased, but didn't say anything.

For several moments the only sound was the fading shriek of the hawk as it drifted away on a thermal.

Then, 'Know what?' Latigo said, suddenly sitting up. 'That's a bunch of hooey.'

'What is?'

'What I said about Gabe. You fellas are dead right. I am jealous of that big ugly sonofabitch. Have been ever since he took up with Ingrid.'

His unusual frankness caught Lawless and Drifter by surprise and neither could think of what to say.

Finally Drifter said, 'Don't feel bad, Lefty,' and exhaled a smoke ring that instantly dissolved in the wind. 'I'm jealous too – 'cept not of Gabe.'

'Who, then?' Lawless asked.

'You, you beef-brain.'

'Me? What the hell you jealous of me for?'

Drifter rolled his eyes as if unable to believe Lawless couldn't guess.

But Latigo knew. 'Yeah, I can see why,' he said. 'Miss Ronnie may not be as flat-out pretty as Ingrid, but there's somethin' special about her that makes up for it. An' she sure as hell is a lot younger.'

'Whoa, hold on, you two,' Lawless exclaimed. 'Let's keep Veronica out of this. She and I—' He got no further as far below them, on the outskirts of Santa Rosa, he glimpsed a rider and a wagon coming along Front Street toward Dr Shaw's house. Quickly raising his glasses, he realized the driver was Sheriff Hansen. Shifting focus, Lawless saw the rider was Luke Otis. The tall, stick-thin deputy carried a shotgun and another shotgun lay on the seat beside the sheriff. Both lawmen were tight-lipped and tense.

Lawless lowered his glasses. 'Get ready to ride,' he told Latigo and Drifter. 'Looks like Hansen's decided to force Doc Shaw's hand.'

'Damn,' Drifter said. 'There's goes our diversion.'

'There's more than one way to trap a skunk,' Lawless said. 'C'mon. . . .'

Rising, the three of them hurried down the slope to their horses, which were feeding on what little brown grass the scorching sun hadn't killed.

CHAPTER NINETEEN

Dr Shaw looked up from his medical logbook as he heard someone enter the waiting room. The sound of boots told him that it was a man – two men, in fact – and before they even came within sight of his open office door, he'd guessed who it was.

'Afternoon, Sheriff – Otis,' he said as both men appeared in his doorway. 'What ails you this bright sunny day?'

'Nothin',' Sheriff Hansen said. 'I'm here on business, Doc.'

'Ahh. You want to talk to Miss Ketchum again, no doubt?'

'No, I'm all talked out, Doc. I've come to arrest her, take her to jail. An' before you tell me she ain't fit to move yet,' he added as Dr Shaw started to protest, 'I'm willin' to accept all responsibility should anything happen to her.'

'I see. . . .' Dr Shaw mopped his sweaty brow with his kerchief. 'Well, then I suppose it's useless to ask you to wait until tomorrow morning—'

'Yep,' Sheriff Hansen said. 'My mind's made up. So save your breath.'

On reaching the bottom of the hill Lawless, Latigo and Drifter spurred their horses into a gallop and entered the outskirts of Santa Rosa from the southwest. A maze of narrow dirt streets led them between the rows of small, run-down adobe hovels that made up 'Mex Town'. Everywhere brown-skinned, dark-eyed, humble-looking men, women and children all stopped what they were doing to watch the three *gringos* ride past. Though the population was still predominantly Mexican, the daily arrival of white settlers by wagon and train was increasing and everyone knew it was just a matter of time before they outnumbered the original inhabitants of the once-sleepy little pueblo.

The sheriff's office faced Front Street and was about midway between Dr Shaw's clinic and the Carlisle Hotel. Lawless, Drifter and Latigo reined up in the alley behind the office, dismounted, tied their horses to a nearby fence and looked about them. No one was in the alley besides themselves and a gaunt, tan mongrel nosing around for food. Satisfied they hadn't been seen, each of them chambered a round into his rifle and moved to the rear door.

'Stay here and keep an eye out,' Lawless told Latigo.

'Why me?'

'Didn't you tell me you were the best who ever lived with a gun?'

'Yeah.'

'There's your answer, *amigo*.' Lawless removed his

142

hat and wiped the sweat from the inner headband before replacing it. 'I doubt if you'll see anyone anyway. I mean, nobody in their right mind would be out in this goddamn heat.'

'In case someone does happen by,' Drifter put in, 'and wants to know why you're here, tell them you're one of Sheriff Hansen's special deputies an' send 'em on their way.'

'An' if they don't believe me?'

'Cold-cock 'em and drag them inside.'

'Shooting 'em would be easier.'

'It would also kill our chances of surprisin' the sheriff and his deputies,' Lawless reminded. 'Then we've got to shoot it out with them an' there'll be no winners when the dust settles.' He nodded for Drifter to follow him and quietly opened the door.

'You're gettin' to sound like a damn politician,' Drifter said once they were inside.

Lawless grinned. 'With Lefty, you got to be diplomatic or else he'll find ten ways to Sunday to argue with you . . . or maybe even shoot you.'

They moved quietly along the narrow hallway that led past the door to the jail area, on into the front office. It was empty and the street door was locked. It was also stifling hot and both men flopped into chairs and fanned themselves with their hats.

'Man, I hate this heat,' grumbled Drifter. 'Makes even the slightest effort seem like a chore.'

'If you hate the heat, how come you bought a ranch outside El Paso? It gets hot as Hades there.'

'Roots.'

'Meanin'?'

'I'm from Texas. So are my kinfolks.'

'Serious?'

'Sure. Why?'

'I always thought you were from Arkansas.'

'Uh-uh.'

'Then why'd you call yourself Arkansas Jack for a spell?'

Drifter grinned sheepishly. 'I liked the name. Way it sounded. I wanted to call myself Arkansas Tom, but I didn't want to be confused with the Arkansas Tom who rides with Bill Doolin.'

'Wise move,' Lawless agreed. 'There's a whole slew of lawmen out to collect the reward on any of Doolin's gang. So where *do* you hail from?' he added.

'Bonham – little eyesore in northeast Texas.

'Bonham?' Lawless frowned. 'Why's that sound familiar?'

'John Wesley Hardin?'

'Oh, that's right. That's where he's from, isn't it? Know Hardin, do you?'

'Sure. Wes an' me went to school together – when we weren't playin' hooky, that is.'

'You still pals?'

'We were never pals. But we do bend an elbow together occasionally.'

'How's that sit with Macahan?'

Drifter shrugged. 'Long as Wes stays out of trouble, Ezra don't mind him around. 'Sides, Wes ain't so wild and ornery now. Doin' time in Huntsville made him see the light. Taught himself to be a lawyer there and then after he was paroled, he moved to El Paso an' hung out a shingle.'

'I heard he does a lot of his lawyerin' in the Acme Saloon?'

'Yeah.' Drifter chuckled. 'Seems Wes forgot they don't allow drinkin' in court an' he needs a little sippin' whiskey if he's goin' to pontificate—' He broke off as horses were heard approaching.

Lawless hurried to the window and looked up the street.

'They're comin',' he told Drifter.

'How many deputies?'

'All of 'em, looks like.'

'Let's hope they're thirsty an' don't all want to bust into this office.'

'We'll be ready either way,' Lawless said, adding: 'Go tell Lefty they're comin' in case they decide to bring that wagon 'round back. We don't want him tipping anyone off that we're in here.'

'Consider it done.' Drifter hurried off to the back door.

Lawless made sure his Colt was fully loaded and then pressed his cheek against the glass. He could now see all of the riders approaching. Led by Sheriff Hansen, with Deputy Otis handling the reins of the wagon carrying Veronica, the twelve heavily armed deputies came riding along Front Street toward the sheriff's office.

It was a chilling sight – and Lawless silently cursed Gabriel Moonlight for not being at his side to help fight the lawmen.

CHAPTER TWENTY

Drifter rejoined Lawless by the window just as Sheriff Hansen, Veronica, Otis and the special deputies reined up in front of the office. Lawless motioned for him to stand on the opposite side of the door and then both waited, rifles cocked, ready to confront anyone who entered.

Outside, Sheriff Hansen noticed the crowd gathering around them. They all looked shocked as they recognized the prisoner and several people called out to Veronica, asking her what had happened. Uneasy, the sheriff ordered his deputies to stop anyone from entering his office. He then dismounted, tied up his horse and offered to help Veronica down from the wagon. Though still a little weak, she defiantly ignored his outstretched hands and climbed down on her own.

'Better put me in irons, sheriff,' she said sarcastically. 'You don't want a criminal as dangerous as me trying to escape while everyone's watching.'

Sheriff Hansen reddened angrily. Ignoring the

amused titter that came from the onlookers, he escorted Veronica into his office.

As the door closed behind him, he saw Lawless and Drifter – and the rifles they were aiming at him – and froze.

'Don't make a sound,' Lawless warned, 'unless you want it to be your last.' Leaning close, he pulled the lawman's Colt from its holster and tossed it in the corner.

'You're makin' a big mistake,' the sheriff said. 'I've got a dozen men outside. One word from me and they'll shoot you down.'

'Could be,' Lawless admitted. 'But you won't live to see it.'

'Lawless, please—' Veronica began.

'Not now, Miss Ronnie,' he said quietly. Going to the desk, he took wrist irons out of the drawer and fastened them around Sheriff Hansen's wrists.

'You'll hang for this,' the lawman said, 'both of you.'

'I wouldn't count on it,' Drifter said.

'If you're expecting Marshal Macahan to help you, forget it. You might be friends, but once he hears how you interfered with the law an' helped a prisoner escape, he'll hunt you two down an' hang you himself!'

Tired of the sheriff's yapping, Lawless slammed his rifle butt against the lawman's head. Stunned, Sheriff Hansen dropped to his knees and slumped over.

'Lawless,' Drifter said sharply, 'that's enough.'

'He does like I tell him,' Lawless said, 'an' he'll

have nothin' to worry about.'

Satisfied, Drifter said: 'What about the horses?'

'You'n Lefty bring them around front. Miss Ronnie an' I will meet you there.'

Drifter nodded and hurried off to the rear door.

Lawless dragged the still-dazed lawman to his feet. 'When we get outside, Will, tell your deputies to throw down their weapons and let us through.'

'Go to hell.'

'Suit yourself,' Lawless said. 'But remember this: the first man who tries to stop us will be the last face you ever see.' To Veronica, he added: 'Once we get outside, I want you to climb up on the wagon. Think you can do that?'

'Y-Yes.'

'Good. You get up there with her,' he told the sheriff, 'and when I tell you, head on out of town. Latigo, Drifter an' me will be right behind you. And if your men have even a lick of brains, they'll do like you told 'em and not try to stop us or follow us. Because if they do there's goin' to be a lot of new widows in Santa Rosa. Clear?'

Head still ringing, Sheriff Hansen grudgingly nodded.

'Stay behind me,' Lawless told Veronica. When she obeyed, he opened the door . . . revealing all the armed deputies.

Jamming his rifle against the sheriff's back, Lawless said: 'Start talkin', Will.'

148

CHAPTER
TWENTY-ONE

Sheriff Hansen nervously licked his lips. 'Listen to me, all of you,' he told his deputies. 'Drop your guns and don't try to stop us from leaving town.'

'But, Will,' Otis began.

'Button it!' the sheriff barked at him. 'Do like I say,' he added to the other men. 'Otherwise, he's goin' to shoot me.'

Otis and the special deputies reluctantly threw down their weapons.

'Now back up and let us through,' Lawless ordered.

Again, the deputies grudgingly obeyed.

Just then Drifter and Latigo came riding around the side of the office, Drifter leading Lawless' line-backed dun.

'Cover 'em,' he said as they reined up beside him. Waiting until they aimed their rifles at the deputies, he then helped Veronica climb on to the wagon. The effort exhausted her and she looked pale and shaky.

'You goin' to be all right, Miss Ronnie?'

'I'll be fine, thanks,' she assured him.

Lawless motioned for the sheriff to climb aboard. The lawman obeyed. Once on the seat beside Veronica, he untied the reins from the brake and waited for Lawless' next instructions.

Lawless stepped up on to his horse and turned to all the mounted deputies. 'Any of you follow us an' you'll need to elect a new sheriff. Clear?'

Otis and the deputies sat there, motionless, glaring at Lawless.

'Get goin', Will,' he told the sheriff.

Teeth gritted, Sheriff Hansen snapped the reins and two horses pulled the creaking wagon on along Front Street.

Kicking up their horses Lawless, Drifter and Latigo escorted it out of town, all of them constantly looking back to make sure they weren't being followed.

It didn't take long to reach the border. There was no fence or sign saying they were entering Mexico; just a large, rocky outcrop that only the locals knew meant they were now in Chihuahua.

Lawless reined up just short of the rocks and told the sheriff to get down. The lawman obeyed. Lawless dismounted, tied his horse to the rear of the wagon, then climbed up beside Veronica.

Sheriff Hansen wagged a warning finger at her. 'You're bein' a darn fool, Miss Ketchum. You go with these men an' you'll spend the rest of your life on the run from the law.'

'I've already come to grips with that,' she said, 'so

150

save the sermon.'

'What about your ranch . . . your livestock?'

'I sent word to Stadtlander that he can buy me out for the right price. Soon as I'm settled in Mexico, I'll hire a lawyer to work out the details.' She smiled at Lawless, who nodded to show his approval.

'Suit yourself, ma'am.' Sheriff Hansen started walking back to town.

'Ready?' Lawless asked Veronica.

'More than ready. . . .' She pressed her hand fondly over his.

Lawless smiled at her and was about to get the wagon rolling, when several gunshots boomed in the distance.

They all looked back in the direction of Santa Rosa and saw a rider racing toward them. Pursuing him were a dozen or more riders, all firing as they rode.

'Jesus,' Lawless said as he recognized the rider. 'It's Gabe.'

'*Now* he shows up,' Latigo grumbled.

'Yeah, an' brings a whole pile of trouble with him,' said Drifter.

Sheriff Hansen, aware that he wasn't being watched, started to run.

Lawless jerked his Colt and fired, the bullet kicking up dirt just ahead of the sheriff's feet. The lawman pulled up sharply and glared at Lawless.

'That's far enough, Will.'

'You two go ahead,' Drifter told Lawless. 'Get Miss Ketchum across the border. Lefty and I'll handle this.'

151

Lawless hesitated, reluctant to leave his friends in a bind.

'Go, goddammit!' Drifter yelled.

Lawless snapped the reins, startling the team into a trot, and the wagon rumbled toward the rocky outcrop.

'Don't worry,' he said, seeing Veronica's concern. 'Soon as we get to those rocks, the law can't touch you.'

She nodded and gave an uneasy smile. Then, as Lawless faced front, she looked back at Gabriel in a way that suggested something other than the law might be troubling her.

CHAPTER TWENTY-TWO

Drifter and Latigo kept their rifles trained on Sheriff Hansen. All three watched as Gabriel galloped toward them, his body hunched over his horse's neck so as not to present a target to the pursuing deputies.

'Tell those bastards to hold their fire,' Drifter told the sheriff. ''Cause if Gabe eats lead, so do you.'

Sheriff Hansen quickly signaled to his deputies to stop shooting.

He was too late. A bullet hit Gabriel's galloping horse and the animal went down like it had been tripped. Gabriel flew over the animal's neck, landed hard and lay in a crumpled heap.

'Sonofa*bitch*,' Latigo said when Gabriel didn't move. Raising his rifle, he snapped off three shots and brought down the three leading deputies. The others reined up, jumped from their horses and took cover behind some rocks.

'You've got ten seconds, Will,' Drifter growled. 'If

153

your boys ain't thrown down their guns by then, I'll put a bullet in your head.'

Alarmed, Sheriff Hansen waved at the deputies, at the same time yelling for them to drop their weapons.

'. . . Seven, six, five, four—' Drifter stopped counting as the deputies threw down their guns.

Just then Lawless came riding up. He didn't stop as he drew level with Drifter and Latigo but galloped on, only stopping when he reached Gabriel.

Dismounting, he kneeled beside his friend. 'You hurt bad?'

Gabriel shook his head and sat up, gasping for air. 'W-Wind,' he wheezed. 'F-Fall . . . knocked all the breath out of me.' He grabbed his hat and rifle and let Lawless help him up. Nearby, his horse was writhing in pain.

Cursing, Gabriel regretfully shot the animal in the head. Then, unfastening his saddle, he slung it over his shoulder and rejoined Lawless. Together they returned to Drifter and Latigo, who sat astride their horses, still covering Sheriff Hansen.

'Sure took your sweet time gettin' here,' Latigo growled at Gabriel.

'Deming's a fair piece, *amigo.*'

'Deming? What the hell were you doin' in New Chicago?'

'Ingrid,' Lawless guessed. 'She must've had business there an' you went with her, right?'

Gabriel ignored the question and turned to Sheriff Hansen, asking: 'Will, do you remember a lawyer by the name of T. C. Rickett?'

'No,' the sheriff lied. 'Why should I?'

' 'Cause, according to Ingrid Bjorkman, he used to have an office in town before he moved to Las Cruces. Sure you don't remember?'

'No. I mean, I dunno. Maybe. Why?'

'He's now in Deming,' Gabriel said. 'Set up practice there. But, then, I don't have to tell you that, do I?'

'Gabe,' Lawless broke in. 'I hate to rush you, Ace, but maybe we ought to discuss this *across* the border?'

Gabriel grinned like he knew a secret. 'When I'm done, *amigo*, chances are you, Drifter and Lefty won't *need* to cross the border. Ain't that right, Will?'

Sheriff Hansen looked uneasy and nervously toed the dirt. 'How the hell should I know?'

'Oh, I dunno,' Gabriel said. 'If a fella married my sister, reckon I'd want to know his whereabouts – 'specially if we were involved in somethin' illegal.'

'Jesus,' Latigo exploded, 'will you get to the goddamn point, Gabe!'

'The point,' Gabriel said, looking toward the rocky outcrop, where Veronica was still seated on the wagon, 'is the sheriff, here, is up to his ass in lies.'

'Damn you,' Sheriff Hansen hissed.

'Shut up an' let him talk,' Lawless said. He followed Gabriel's gaze and realized he was looking at Veronica. 'If it has anythin' to do with Miss Ronnie, I want to hear it.'

' 'Fraid it does,' Gabriel said. 'See, her daddy hired Mr T.C. Rickett to handle some business 'tween him and Stadtlander. Had to do with a contract dealin' with the water rights to the Lower Snake—' He broke off as the sheriff grabbed Latigo's leg and tried to pull him from the saddle. Before he could, Drifter swung his rifle and clubbed the lawman, sending him sprawling in the dirt.

'Hold it, Lefty!' Lawless said as Latigo went to shoot the sheriff. 'We need the bastard alive. Go on,' he added to Gabriel. 'Finish your piece.'

'You may not like what you hear,' Gabriel warned.

'Tell me anyway, Ace.'

Gabriel shrugged. 'Well, seems Miss Ketchum paid Will, here, and the lawyer a bunch of money to keep the whereabouts of said contract a secret.'

'Is that right, Will?' Lawless demanded.

The sheriff's guilty look told everyone it was.

'So . . . Stadtlander wasn't lyin' after all.'

'I'll be a dirty. . . .' Drifter muttered.

'Well, well, well,' Latigo said softly. 'Who would've figured. . . ?'

'I had no choice,' the sheriff blurted. 'Said she'd tell everyone that the votin' was rigged, and how Stadtlander's money had bought me my star.'

'And you couldn't have that, could you?' Gabriel said, ' 'cause then all the folks around here would've demanded another vote an' you would've lost the election no matter *who* ran against you.'

Sheriff Hansen lowered his eyes and didn't say anything.

Lawless suddenly said: 'I'll be right back.' He leapt into the saddle and dug his heels in. The horse broke into a canter that quickly carried Lawless to the border . . . across into Mexico.

Latigo, Drifter, Gabriel and Sheriff Hansen watched as Lawless reached the wagon. Remaining mounted, he spoke briefly to Veronica. She argued vehemently, but couldn't change Lawless' mind. Grasping the reins, he led the horses and wagon back on to U.S. soil and reined up beside the sheriff, who was now standing.

'Here,' he said, tossing the reins to the lawman. 'You two deserve each other.'

'Lawless, please,' Veronica begged. 'Give me a chance to explain.'

'Save your lies for Stadtlander,' Lawless said. 'I'm sure he'll be a better listener.' Before she could argue, he added to the sheriff: 'You want to keep that tin star, Will, make sure Miss Ketchum tells Stadtlander the truth.'

Sheriff Hansen nodded. He then climbed on to the wagon beside Veronica and shook out the reins.

'Hold on,' Gabriel said quickly. 'I need one of them horses.' He unhooked the horse on the right side of the wagon tongue, saddled it and swung up on to its back.

The sheriff snapped the reins over the remaining horse and the wagon rolled off toward the deputies.

Lawless looked after Veronica for a painful moment, then released his feelings in a long, resigned sigh.

Gabriel fondly gripped Lawless' shoulder. 'Sorry, *amigo*.'

'Don't be. You did me a big favor. I was pretty nigh roped by that gal.'

'Not hard to understand,' Drifter said. 'Most of us would've gladly taken your place.'

'Yeah, well,' Lawless said. 'Live an' learn, right?'

There was a moment of awkward silence. Then: 'I don't know 'bout you three,' he continued, 'but right now I need to get acquainted with a bottle of tequila.'

'Maybe even two or three bottles,' said Latigo.

'Now you're talkin',' Drifter said. 'I'm goin' to get drunker than a hoot owl 'fore I head back to El Paso.'

'If you ain't particular about company,' Lawless said, 'me an' Lefty will join you.'

'My pleasure, gents.'

'An' afterwards, you can all sleep it off at my place,' Gabriel said. 'Latigo knows how to get there.'

' 'Mean you ain't comin'?' said Lawless.

'Hell, no. I've done enough hard ridin' for a spell. 'Sides, I promised Ingrid I'd tell her how it all turned out.'

'Smooth as Sunday,' Lawless said. 'Oh, and while you're tellin' her, be sure to give that pretty lady a big hug for me.'

'Like hell I will,' Gabriel scowled.

'But she saved me from makin' a damn fool of myself.'

'I don't give a damn *what* she saved you from. You want to hug someone, *amigo*, hug one of them Mex whores you plan on swiggin' tequila with.'

'All right. Then at least tell Ingrid how grateful I am.'

'An' have her like you more than she does already? No, thanks.' Nodding goodbye to Latigo and Drifter, Gabriel kicked up his horse and rode off.

'Can you believe that?' Lawless said incredulously.

Drifter shook his head. 'In all the years I've known Gabe, I never knew he had a jealous streak.'

'Me neither.'

'Maybe next time,' Latigo said smugly, 'you'll listen to me.'

' 'Bout what?'

'Gabe not bein' sure of himself.'

Lawless and Drifted exchanged puzzled looks.

'What the hell you talkin' about, Lefty?'

'I said all along that Gabe knows he ain't good enough for Ingrid.'

'No, you didn't. You never said nothin' of the sort. What you said was, you didn't know what she saw in him.'

'Same thing.'

'Ain't the same thing at all.'

'Sure it is.'

'Ain't.'

'Jesus, here we go again,' grumbled Drifter. 'Both of you, carryin' on like a grouchy ol' married couple.'

Lawless and Latigo started to protest, then both saw the funny side of it and broke out laughing. It was contagious and Drifter joined in.

'Palomas, here we come,' Latigo crowed.

Lawless raised his hand as if in toast. 'To red-lipped whores an' light-footed cowboys.'

'An' tequila,' chimed in Drifter. 'Rivers of it!'

'Amen,' they all said together.

Laughing, the three of them kicked up their horses and rode across the border into Mexico.